...There was no movement that he could see, nothing besides the coursing of his blood that his ears could hear. Faintly the images of the deadened androids in the yard became recognizable and, after telling himself that if he didn't move now it was all over but the screaming, he ran for the back door.

Down the curb, over the thin layer of tarmac, up again, and he stumbled over a leg, sprawled with hands groping toward nothing. His shoulder struck a head. There was a century of panic as he struggled to release himself from the corpselike grip of one of Coates' children, standing, stepping away, and falling again, this time to reach out and grip the unyielding breast of someone's android wife. His palms, lips, forehead slick with perspiration as he rolled over onto his hands and knees and crawled to the door, unlocked it, and fell inside into a deeper blackness...

THE SHADOW OF ALPHA

C.L. Grant

A BERKLEY MEDALLION BOOK

published by

BERKLEY PUBLISHING CORPORATION

For Sydney and Minerva, who gave me Me;
For John and Barbara, who gave me Her;
And the first, here the last:
Debbie, who gave me Always.

Kirby McCauley
220 East 26th Street
New York, N.Y. 10010

SBN 425-03143-8

BERKLEY MEDALLION BOOKS are published by
Berkley Publishing Corporation
200 Madison Avenue
New York, N.Y. 10016

BERKLEY MEDALLION BOOK ® TM 757,375

Printed in the United States of America

Berkley Medallion Edition, JUNE, 1976

THE
SHADOW
OF
ALPHA

One

On a summer warm morning, Parric stood on the narrow, functionally ornamented porch of his three-room home and wondered what would happen to the universe should he decide to skip a day at the clinic and stay in bed, the better to count the holes in his head he must have had when he accepted this job in the first place. Grinning sardonically to himself, he composed a scenario of the cataclysmic consequences his nonattention to the salvation of the human race would produce: the World of Finance would no doubt totter, teeter, and eventually unimpressively implode, throwing millions out of work, nations into war, and computers into red-blinking hysteria. Not to mention, he reminded himself, a World of Politics that would rumble, grumble, and swing into convulsive inaction behind the stumbling vanguard of a thousand newly formed investigatory committees. Science would shudder into classic testtube breakdowns, Philosophy would begin muttering to itself in tongues not even the thinkers would understand, and the Arts would write itself a twelve-act, highly symbolic trivid operatic drama that would cast him as a sensuously sinister combination of Mephistopheles and the Whore of Babylon.

"I think," he said to the shadows drawing from him, "I need a vacation."

He sat, then, on the topmost of the porch's four steps to await patiently the jagged saw of sanctioned lightning that would surely strike him to a cinder for his heresy; he waited long enough to realize that he was still quite alone.

"Fat chance I'd get hit anyway," he decided, speaking with weary bitterness to the curves of his knees. "With my luck, I'd only get singed bald."

He leaned back on his elbows, heedless of the dust gathering to his dark, loose-fitting shirt, and squinted a brief surveillance through the bright light. The Town, nameless, was silent when most towns in most sectors were blaring their way past sunrise into another, sometime productive, working day; and unlike most other communities, Parric's Town was clean, shaded, neatly appointed with half-remembered greenery and sterile but well-meaning attempts at color-life gardens. The entire project had been conceived, plotted, and programmed in less than two decades, and his own portion was then constructed between foothills that formerly permitted only a stream to split them. That stream yielded now to the main street, and most of the low, broad-leaved trees had been summarily replaced by six blocks of single-story buildings blastpainted and prettified to maintain illusions of a community alive.

In a city that Parric preferred to forget existed, the Town was a number that printed out in four digits, followed by a series of relentlessly stubborn graphs which, according to those who read them, proved conclusively that man was finally ready to embark upon the solemn millennium of a nearly embalmed utopia.

But away from the magnetic tapes and weekly pep

talks, Parric recognized the Town for what it was, no matter how often he was admonished by his employers to forgo his cynical responses to their evaluation questionnaires.

Façade.

Nothing more.

Behind every house, three to a block, was a yard, and behind every yard was a shimmering tri-sectioned barrier that one could see only if the light was right and the angle just so. Nothing but air passed through in either direction, and beyond were the hills that wrenched their way through the seasons as if the Town hadn't been there at all.

The main street, the side streets: to follow them the few short meters from the ends of the Town, and they stopped. Dead. Without even the dignity of fading into a trail.

"Ah, well," said Parric as he had each morning for nearly a year, and he rose, grabbed the briefcase he had toted from the kitchen, and began his walk to work.

The sun was a white-yellow bright, and a breeze hushed around him; above him in the fat-boled trees crowned a gleaming green. On the sidewalk were evidences of a night's light rainfall occasioned by Climat-Con: angular puddles suspending shards of bark, blades of mown grass and twisted weak twigs that could not hang on long enough to be trimmed by Maintenance. The neighborhood, for the most part, was silent, but now and then he could hear the muffled cries of women summoning children, sprightly music to those who might have overslept. He saw Dan Bonetto bending awkwardly over a patch of garden by the side of his house, and he made a note. Willard Dix waved halfheartedly from his front yard, and Parric nodded. Two children scampered from behind a low hedge into the trafficless street, calling to him, and Parric answered with a grin.

Waking, the Town prepared to play a charade.

Façade.

But more often than not, Parric realized, what he had now was infinitely better, or so he liked to believe, than what had been just a year ago, and he used the time he spent walking to the clinic to remind himself of it as forcefully as he could.

He was sitting at his cubiclelike desk watching the rolling, interhouse comunit flash actuarial statistics when a Secretary, silver-rimmed black and as officious as a machine could get, slid into the huge office and blinked over the heads of the two dozen other clerks who were hunched over their occupations in mirror mime of Parric's own attitude. He paid little attention to the quietly humming robot, anticipating nothing as others usually did when it hove into their sanctuary. If not exactly inspired, Parric was nevertheless conscientious, and Everlasting Life Assurance, an innocuously steady noneminence in the field, had never had a complaint since he had joined the firm directly out of the training school it had paid him to attend. It was, then, a more than unsettling moment when the Secretary rolled silently to his desk and waited until he looked up.

"Franklin Parric?" The voice, recorded and re-simulated to sound like a pleasant woman dying for a place to spend the night, instantly reminded him of the sirens who hummed sailors to death on a continent he had only seen in an atlas.

He nodded an affirmative and pushed away from his

work, punching the screen on "hold" until, or if, the machine would leave him with his employment intact.

"There is a request that you take the first available opportunity from your duties, Mr. Parric, and report to Mr. Coates in Personnel. There will be no need for you to summon a replacement. Your position will be filled from the pool."

The Secretary took his stuttering to be a dismissal and glided out as swiftly as it had arrived.

At the Town's only major intersection, four roads that led nowhere but preserved the ghostly ties with the outside world, Parric noticed his hands were perspiring as they had that day he had been mustered out of his office-to-home life. He remembered thinking in frantic circles about losing his apartment, his books, his food, his clothing, his unenthusiastic taste for life, and suddenly recalled how he had begun insanely calculating the height of the nearest walkway bridge.

You poor sap, he thought as he crossed the street, laughing aloud and startling himself with the explosion of noise in the silence. What was it they used to say: Had I but known?

Floyd Coates was short, flirting with jowls and trussed into a tunicsuit that might have made him appear slimmer had he had the proper tailor. Coates, however, was also parsimonious about the way he applied his finances to his appearance and thus looked as if he had taken a razor to a bedsheet. His eyes always appeared rabbit-wide frightened, never narrowing even in a frown, which now multiplied his facial folds as Parric stepped through the door that slid aside for him at his knock.

"Frankie," in a voice that grated like nails gently tracing over metal, "sit down, son, and light yourself something if you smoke."

Parric sat gingerly on the edge of an old-style static chair, but only smiled his refusal of a cigar that was handed to him over a clear-topped expanse that separated him from his potential executioner. Coates nodded, flipped open a microfile, and inserted a spool, dwarfed by finger and thumb, into an overly elaborate console at his side. Parric watched in fascination as the hooded screen cast a hue over his supervisor's face as unearthly as the dream he felt himself in.

"Frankie, you've been with us for nearly a dozen years now, and a fine round twelve that's been, too."

"Thank you, Mr. Coates."

"We've never had words, that I can remember, and you've always been willing to put in a little overtime here and there to help Everlasting out."

Parric thought of the bills that waited in ambush whenever he returned to his room-and-a-half castle, and shrugged deprecatingly. As the man continued the examination of whatever the console was showing him, Parric was reminded of a bear that couldn't wait for spring before replenishing fat lost during hibernation; his hands pressed hard against his knees, but he couldn't stop his shoulders from trembling.

"Well, Frankie, in grateful thanks for all you've done for us, I'm going to give you the opportunity to get loose from us."

"Loose?" Parric straightened, his obsequious servant pose shattering at his feet. "What does that mean? You're firing me? Demotion? What?"

"Wait a minute, Franklin," Coates said, waving a thick-fingered hand to protect himself from Parric's

6

sudden anger. "We are not going to fire you. There's no cause. No cause at all. What we will do, however, is, well . . . I'm not really sure how to phrase it because the situation is, to say the least, unusual. But . . . let's start with loan and see what happens."

"No offense, Mr. Coates," Parric said, "but you're not making very much sense. You're going to loan me, or give me a loan? Loan me? To Whom? For what?"

The clinic was the only nonresidence in the Town, a square brown-and-white box with hinged windows and a door that hissed to one side when the welcome mat was trod upon. At the angle where lawn and sidewalk met was a plain white post from which an arm extended, dangling a rectangular black sign proclaiming the Clinic office of Franklin Y. Parric, MD. Parric flicked out a finger as he passed, watched the shingle swing gently before hurrying up the walk to insert the key that activated the entrance.

The waiting room was blandly furnished, could have been bare, and he stayed only long enough to thumb open the windows to air out the panel-enclosed space. If, he thought, he had received anything at all from his new life, it was the desire for continuing fresh air, air that arrived unbottled and reasonably untampered with direct from the atmosphere to the consumer. There were times, quiet hours during the early evening when he felt the loneliness the most, when he did nothing else but walk the streets breathing unfettered, so unique was the experience, so exhilarating the sensations.

And the back of the building was his workshop.

"Frankie, it will come as no surprise to you, working

with the figures in your department as you do, that the world's death rate has been climbing alarmingly over the past generation; a rate which, if continued, will not do us a heck of a lot of good in the foreseeable future. Needless to say, a lot of economies, including our own, could be in for a big crunch. Those PopCon folks sure did a hell of a job, didn't they?''

"Excuse me, Mr. Coates, but I'll have to disagree with you there. PopCon isn't entirely to blame. They only accelerated what probably would have happened anyway.''

"I know, Frankie, I know and stand corrected. Bear with me then, and jump in whenever I stray again. If your reports are correct, and I'm sure they are, figures indicate that by the time populations had stabilized to an uncomfortable but tolerably high level, there were too many other factors that most people didn't plan on, or just plain ignored in the hopes that they'd somehow vanish. Pollution in industrial centers rippled certain biological effects such as the increase in incidence of certain new strains of cancers we were unable to control quickly enough, much less identify in the beginning; refusal of places like India and the Central African Union to pay adequate attention to farm improvement implementation, which resulted in massive overloads and eventual soil nutrition depletion that progressed too rapidly for synthetics to match; the, uh, the . . . how many wars were there?''

"Six,'' Parric said, thinking of the last, from which he had been spared because of age when the Continental Draft was reinstated.

"Six,'' Coates repeated, turning from the screen and staring at him. "Son, you've been telling us for

8

years that something ought to be done or we might not be around long enough to find out how the Starship fared.''

"The *Alpha*," Parric said, believing the dignity of the momentous project was sullied without its proper name. "I'll tell you, I wish I had been smart enough to try out for it. You know, Mr. Coates, I'm not an active person, far from it, but there must be some way we can make the government, any government for that matter, see what we're heading for. Promises are fine when some joker's running for office, but don't you think there's something our industry can do to make them see beyond that?"

Coates smiled and handed him a cigar.

Parric dropped his briefcase into a corner and lifted a white smock from the back of a static chair he seldom used. His desk, utilitarian and small, was uncluttered, the bottom two drawers of a curiously outdated filing cabinet empty. The walls were undecorated and could have been blue except for the green one saw when not looking directly at them. It was comfortable, however, and Parric didn't mind having an office all to himself after so many years of staring at the backs and heads of men he had never taken the time to meet. Checking his watch against the desk chronometer, he nodded and shuffled a handful of folders from the cabinet before opening the closet and huffing out a diagnostic unit nearly two meters high and half again as wide. After activation and a quick review/check, it settled its cylindrical bulk and waited, as Parric did, for the first patient.

"You know something," he said to the unit as he

stared out the rear window at the forest that rose higher than he could see without bending, "I think I'm getting a headache. Maybe I should take the day off and try some fishing. Assuming, of course, that there are still fish out there somewhere."

A chime whisper-smooth interrupted his rebellion in thought, and he turned around to greet Mrs. Keller.

There had been thirty-five men besides himself chosen at random for their low profiles: average ambition, drive, and intelligence, reliable loyalty potential, and the fact that none had had the commitment urge to make more than token attachments to the world at large. They were flown to Sector Capital Washington, mildly protesting but more attentively intrigued, where they were checked and checked again for possible security breaches, though none had ever been in a position to do more than simply survive. Handsome salaries and promises of future security damped their uneasiness while they were bottle-fed information about the Towns and their inhabitants.

And were told: as populations dropped slowly toward the levels of the end of the first industrial age, man discovered that the so-called good life and its trinkets were not all that was dreamt of in poetry and prose. With more for everyone, there was, increasingly, less of everyone to enjoy it.

Factor number one, it was stressed, was the need to create a larger consumer base, or industry would falter, people would lose their time-consuming jobs, and there would be starvation and apathy in the midst of plenty.

Factor number two, which Parric more readily understood that the economics, was the emergence of a

*psychological dependency on neighbors. Ironically,
the overcrowding of earlier centuries had developed
within many the need for people close by. At the same
time, several countries began to see the tempting
availability of more and more land for their citizens;
and from the year 2004, six wars of varying sizes,
intense in their medieval dedication to the absorption of
borders, caused the largest nations to realize that man-
power was becoming too valuable to waste.*

*Though the itch remained, the way to scratch it had
to be altered.*

*While governments planned, one way or another, to
increase their populations.*

Parric lifted a folder from the pile on his desk,
thinking he should call Cameron McLeod in a Town
farther up the line and invite him to dinner. Mrs. Keller
always affected him that way, and Cam's raucously
genial company was the only known antidote.

"Right on time, lovely lady," he said, scanning the
graphs that made his eyes water in their complexity.
"Correction, five minutes early. But if you'll just prepare yourself as usual, Mrs. Keller, we'll get under
way. The short routine today."

He looked up, smiling, and froze his arm in the act of
reaching for the diagunit's primary appendages.

"You," he said, "are not Mrs. Keller."

The woman standing in the doorway shook her head,
puzzled and amused by his startled reaction. She was
shorter than his own less than average height, blonde to
his brown, and a little more slender than he would have
molded had he been her designer. She wore a reporter's
elongated singlet, fringed, flared at the knees where her
black boots began, and girdled with red and encum-

bered with various cases carrying the recording devices of her profession.

"Unless I'm talking to a machine," she said, "you must be Franklin Parric, right?"

"My God," he said, placing the folder none too gently on the desk behind him. "You're human."

Chapter 2

A microsecond of panicked thought that he was about to be replaced was superseded by the irritating realization that he must look the complete fool staring as he was.

"Listen," she said while he vacillated between directionless anger and surprise, "didn't they tell you I was coming?"

Immediately, he decided to get angry and, oblivious to the fact that he was not performing his duties as the Town's premier host, glared at her before striding around the desk and punching at a consolet recessed next to the chronometer. He looked up once, saw her smiling patiently, and frowned, The tiny embedded screen finally shimmered a picture he could barely see. But he knew well enough he was facing Floyd Coates, now firmly entrenched in a bigger office in a bigger building in the capital of the country that had pressed him precipitously into its service.

"Damnit, Floyd," he said, "what's going on around here?"

"Ah, Frankie, and may I assume that little Jessica

Windsor has arrived at your quaint little resort in the mountains?''

Parric began a nervous tapping on the screen with a fingernail. ''There is a lady here who, I suppose, has a name like Windsor. She hasn't bothered to introduce herself. But that's beside the point, confound it. I want to know what she's doing here scaring me half to death popping in like she did without warning. And while I'm at it, Floyd, how did she get in without my knowing it?''

Despite the inconvenient size of the unreliable comunit, he saw the supervisor break into a bear's grin, and he snapped the connection without waiting for a reply. Coates, he thought, was getting a little too involved with his newfound authority.

''Tell me something,'' the woman said, approaching the desk with something less than her original good humor, ''are you always like this? So friendly, I mean.''

''Miss Windsor, and I presume that's who you are,'' he said as she nodded, ''I am only like this when things happen to upset my equilibrium. At precisely 0907, Mrs. Angeline Keller is supposed to walk in here, take off her clothes, and let me check her out. When Mrs. Angeline Keller does not walk in here and someone else does, what do you expect me to do?''

''Try asking me to sit down.''

''If you're expecting me to cringe and become suddenly apologetic, forget it, Miss Windsor. There's a chair over there, and you can sit if you want. I have work to do.''

Jessica stared, then carted the indicated chair from the corner and sat, her hands clasped a strained white in her lap. Parric leaned involuntarily away from the broiling contempt in her expression, his initial anger washing away the shock and fading with it. He had had enough surprises during the past few months and believed himself adequately entitled to a ration of indignation.

"I have a feeling," he finally said, "that with all that gear there, you must be some kind of an investigator and will get around soon enough to telling me just why you are here. But if you don't mind, I'd like to ask a question first: how did you get in without triggering the alarms?"

For a moment, she only toyed with the fluffed fringe on her sleeve, then slid a ringless hand into a breast pocket and pulled out a red-and-yellow serrated triangle of metaglass. She held it up to him, without smiling, and Parric instantly patted his thigh, feeling a similar patchkey still in his pocket. He nodded and puffed his cheeks before blowing a sigh, resigned in the realization that this Jessica Windsor was either a very, very important person, or knew quite a few people who were.

Some four hundred and fifty meters below the clinic there hummed (he liked to think, though knowing there was silence) a fusion generator that perpetuated a triple-screen quadramolecular shield which effectively domed the Town. Entry and exit was generally impossible unless power was reduced or one had a temporary breaker like his. Forceable attempts at penetration would have sounded enough alarms to scare even the machines. Those birds and small animals left in the vicinity had long ago learned to avoid it; and as it was selectively permeable, air filtered through it, was cleansed and made sufficiently breathable to negate the necessity for the masks that were still standard in the more densely populated sections of the country. The power, he knew, was formidable and explained, in simple terms to his unscientific mind, why more of them had not been created over the cities: the danger of leakage, breakdowns, and explosions were sufficient enough, though statistically remote, to prevent the most ardent supporters from swaying the general populace. The latter would, so went a popular campaign slogan of three decades back, rather be filtered than fried.

And up until now, only those intimately involved with the project were allowed free access to the Towns.

Parric was reluctantly impressed, and immediately wondered if his friend McLeod was undergoing the same ordeal.

He smiled, badly.

"Miss Windsor," he said, "there are a few minutes yet before the real Mrs. Keller arrives, so you might as well start with whatever it is you have to do."

She shrugged carelessly, settled herself as best she could in the plastahemp webbing of the chair, and brushed a hand through a waterfall of hair that kept sifting over her right eye. Parric thought the effect was ludicrous.

"Mr. Parric, your Mr. Coates, and others, of course, have decided that sometime in the future there has to be some sort of history written about the project, presumably to be published only after its widespread success. Not the kind of history that the usual article hacks can steal from a printout or pamphlet, but a subjective experience kind of thing that will hopefully make the entire affair a little more acceptable to the country at large. Most of it, and I have to admit to some prejudice

16

here myself, does not exactly take to living side by side with robots."

"Wrong from the start, Miss Windsor," Parric said, though not as forcefully as he would have liked, simultaneously cursing himself for his meekness. "Androids are not robots except in the strictest sense of the word. They are completely self-contained, give or take a century or two, and have synthesized biological systems that would put to shame most of our homegrown ones. They can be, and are, in fact, programmed to such an exact degree as to make them virtually indistinguishable from the real thing without cutting through the flesh, if you'll pardon the expression. A layman would have to be damned careful before making a judgment. Mostly, if you want to know a trade secret, it's in the eyes."

She said nothing, did nothing, and Parric wondered if she were listening at all. He stopped, waited, but was forestalled in expanding his lecture by another chime.

"Customer," he said, rising. "Watch, and maybe you'll learn something."

"You know," she said as she dragged her chair behind the desk and sat again, pointedly pushing his to one side, "you're awfully cocky for an insurance clerk. Do those things really scare you that much?"

He almost nodded, caught himself just as a puffing, stereotyped matron rushed into the office, already fussing with the buttons of a trousered outfit he thought might have been appropriate had she been twenty years younger-looking and seventy pounds lighter.

"Good morning, Dr. Parric," she said, her arms trying to contort behind her to loosen the garment. "Lovely day, isn't it?"

"Absolutely, Mrs. Keller, but a bit warm for my taste, if you don't mind me saying so. By the way, I hope you won't be too bothered, but we have a visitor from the outside today." He nodded toward Jessica, who smiled as Mrs. Keller waved a pudgy forefinger.

"For heaven's sake, why should I mind? I only wish I was her size again."

She laughed, Jessica joined her, and Parric sullenly reached for a scalpel-like instrument resting in a side drawer of a diagunit.

"Will this take long, doctor? I do have a dozen things to do today. You should have seen the mess the children left in the house before they went outside to play. You'd think they weren't at all brought up properly. Sometimes I wonder why I bother, I really do. Ouch, that's cold!"

Parric had separated her upper garment and had inserted the scalpel into a hairthin line that, once violated, automatically split to her shoulderblades and folded neatly down to the base of her spine.

"Mrs. Keller, how many children do you have?"

"Two, the little darlings, but I don't know what to do with them when they get like they do. Do you have children, uh, Miss—"

Parric efficiently untelescoped primary leads from the diagunit and connected them to several spiraled nipples in Mrs. Keller's workings.

"Jessica. Jessica Windsor."

"Jessica. Nice. I approve. Are you married, Jessica?"

"Was," she said, and Parric looked away from his readings in time to see her smile tighten fractionally.

"Sorry," Mrs. Keller said. "Too nosy is my problem, though heaven knows there isn't much to learn

18

around here. Frank can tell you that, can't you, doctor?''

"Mrs. Keller makes the absolute best organic meals in the country," Parric said as he instituted a relay that would feed the necessary information into the diagunit's network link. "How are you feeling, Mrs. Keller? No more dizziness?''

"Gracious, no. Whatever it was you stuck in there last week made things just fine, just fine. Sparkling is how I feel. By the way, did you know there's a strange little man outside? I think he's taking pictures. Will I get on the trivid?''

"Could be. He's my assistant," Jessica said before Parric could ask.

"All right, Mrs. Keller, we're done. And you can tell the others not to worry.''

She nodded, waited with head down until he had refastened her skin, and rushed out without saying goodbye.

Parric remained silent as he reset the machine for the next patient and dropped Mrs. Keller's file back into the drawer. When he was finished, he sat on the edge of the desk.

"What's his name?''

She grinned. "If you're looking for more surprises, don't bother. He's the only other one. Ike Lupozny, by the way. A nice guy, if you like guys singlehandedly trying to revive the ancestral art of gum chewing.''

Parric frowned, not exactly sure whether or not she was trying to goad him toward another brink of self-revelation. The fact that she had nearly forced him to admit to someone other than himself that the androids unnerved him was annoying; even after ten months, he continually had to remind himself that the simulacra were just that and nothing more. Coates, he was positive, had been well aware of his irrational fear, but the supervisor had said nothing throughout the final screening. For some reason, the man had taken a liking to him, and Parric now knew what friends in high places meant.

"Miss Windsor—"

"Listen, would you mind calling me Jess, or Jessie, or Jessica, or even hey you?"

Parric lifted his palms in a shrug. "Whatever you say, lady. You're the boss, it seems. But I would like to know what your plans are." He stumbled, felt as if he were falling through a colorless gel that would not permit him to do anything but spin whenever he tried to swim. Unlike most of the present human race, he had concluded that being alone was not as bad as many had made it out to be. There were, especially during the dark hours, times when the sound of a human voice from a womb-developed larynx would have been worth its reception in gold; but people frightened him more than the androids did. Lesser of a million evils, he thought, but was not convinced.

"Are you going to listen—can I call you Frank?—or do I have to send you a post?"

He started, grinned inanely, and was relieved when the chime sounded again.

Jessica grimaced her annoyance. "Does this go on for very long?"

"Most of the day," he said. "They come in for varying degrees of checks three times a week."

"How many are there, for crying out loud?"

"Forty-seven."

For once she seemed impressed by something he had said, and it rankled him to feel pleased, trying as he was not to develop grandeurs or notions of self-deification.

"That," he said, unable to control himself, "counts the children and mainenance crews. It doesn't include me."

"I wonder," she muttered as old man Dix shuffled in, preventing Parric from responding.

"Pretty," Dix said when he was introduced to Jessica, but afterward remained silent despite attempts to draw him into a conversation that soon became totally one-sided. Parric frowned, double-checked his previous week's report and answers from Central before letting him go.

"Trouble?" Jessica asked.

"Some. He too much plays the role somehow. I keep threatening to send him to a less-tolerant Town, but it doesn't do any good. I'm no mechanic, see, so I have to depend on the Central to either send me instructions for repairs or a completely reprogrammed cell." He tugged at his earlobe and waved her silent before she could launch another spate of questions. "Listen," he said, "I'm no genius and this stuff sometimes gets confusing unless I can think between patients. Would you mind just watching and we can talk later?"

She considered, smiled, and sat back to observe, saying little, opening up only when the scheduled patients found her willing to talk about more than how warm it was, how cool it was, how lovely are the hills this time of year. Her casual gregariousness upset him, and Parric soon found himself abandoning his own dialogue in favor of "Strip," "Close," and "See you Wednesday."

Façade, he thought. Someone was trying to create depth where none existed.

And: why the hell doesn't she go bother McLeod?

And he fought himself until the last patient left them alone at 1600. He waited until the Central confirmed receipt of his data, then dropped his token white into the closet with the diagunit before closing and locking the windows. When she asked him who was around to steal anything, he only grunted, held open the front door as she passed, and stepped outside to make a show of securing it. Standing on the sidewalk was Ike Lupozny.

Parric's initial reaction was amazement at his age, much too old to be carrying around a bulky trivid camerapak on his shoulder. His hair was thin and white, brushed straight back and slicked to curl up at the nape of his neck. His face, however, betrayed his youth, and Parric assumed the pronounced stoop must have been the result of the equipment he used. And it wasn't long before he knew what Jessica meant about the chewing. Lupozny somehow managed to keep a huge wad of gum at the side of his mouth without losing any clarity of pronunciation. It was, Parric realized, an expensive habit and it only reinforced his belief that this particular pair had not been chosen for their assignment quite as randomly as he; they must have been specific choices, and the idea depressed him.

"You run this all by yourself, Frank?" Ike asked as they walked down the center of the street toward Parric's home. "Must take a lot of work."

"It runs itself," Parric said reluctantly. "All I do is watch."

"No cars?"

"None. The Town is too small for them. There's one called the Central that has a larger plant. That one is complete with all the trimmings."

Jessica walked silently beside him, her head cocked toward his shoulder, her eyes watching the road, darting now and then to follow a movement in one of the yards or along one of the streets. Several of the inhabitants called out, inviting Parric and his friends to dinner, but Parric declined, politely, and received only one insulted glare.

"What's that one's name, Dix?"

"Glad you remember," Parric said, not quite able to keep the sarcasm out of his smile. "He's so unfriendly, sometimes I argue with him just to remind myself what people can be like." He grinned this time at Jessica's frown, bowed mockingly as he slid open the door, and allowed them to enter his home first.

They stood for a moment in a claustrophobic foyer, examining without offering the socially acceptable murmurs of faint praise. Ahead of them was the kitchen, to the left the living room, which he entered quickly while pointing the way to a door at the far corner. "My room," he said and stood aside while they unloaded their equipment and tested the bed he hadn't bothered to slip back into the wall. Leaning against the jamb, he watched at the easy way they moved, staying arm's length from each other yet defining an intimacy he immediately begrudged. There were night thoughts flickering through his mind, but he dismissed them as being none of this business.

Time, and dinner was quickly served since Parric hadn't bothered to accumulate the natural foodstuffs offered him by the Central. He was used to and somehow preferred the synthetics the ovenwall produced within minutes of his directions. Despite the impression he had allowed Jessica to foster, Mrs. Keller's cooking was not all that exciting. Whoever had programmed her apparently had a passion for spices that his stomach forbore to cultivate.

They spoke little while eating, a consensus soon arrived at when Ike, his voice stentorian even while whispering, announced his intention to prowl with his camera through the nightlife of the Town. Accordingly, he ate quickly, his face not bothering to disguise his distaste for the food, or for the ale which Parric preferred dark and warm. And when he had vanished, Parric swept the table clean and retreated to the porch, Jessica joining him after changing into a shift with subtly kaleidescoping patterns that kept him from staring too long at her figure.

"Nice," she said, leaning against the railing and nodding toward his chest. He looked down at his shirt, billowing at waist and sleeves to provide him with maximum comfort and coolness. It was typically his, unembroidered and black, making him seem heavier than he was. When he returned his gaze to her face, she grinned. "Really. I like it. Too many men are getting too damn fancy. Those slashed-look shirts and painted-on doublets . . . the kilts I suppose I can live with, but when they wear pants that look more like skin than cloth—" She laughed and looked at him again as if praising him for his conservatism. "They say these things move in cycles, but sometimes I wonder."

There was laughter, friendly, and Parric saw Ike talking with Dan Bonetto, who was gesticulating excitedly around his garden.

"What exactly do you do around here, Frank?"

Parric eased his hand out of his pocket and rubbed the back of his neck. "When you ask me like that, it doesn't seem like a heck of a lot. Observe, mostly. The doctor business is all for show and, I guess, to give me some misguided sense of importance. The times when

I'm not at the clinic, I walk around talking, sitting, making sure there's nothing out of kilter."

"Kilter?"

He smiled at her puzzlement over the old word, relaxing enough to sit on the steps and fold his arms around his knees. "Malfunction, I guess it means. For example, if an android falls down unexpectedly, he damned well better show he's in some kind of pain or look surprised or anything else a human would do in such a situation. Reactions, then, are mainly what I am supposed to keep track of. What it factors out to be is that they have to be perfect and imperfect at the same time."

She sat beside him and he eased carefully to the edge of the step, creating a gap she could not have ignored, instantly contrite that he had done it and too unsure to rectify his move.

"It's frightening, in a way," she said, staring through a veil of dusk as the hills with their stunted trees and ragged crests sliced off the orange setting sun. "People should know what they're living with."

"Supposedly they will, in time. Right now, though, these androids are needed to punch production."

She laughed, lightly, quickly. "Sounds like Floyd talking."

"It is, I guess. You listen to that growling long enough, you start to growl yourself. He's right, though, I think. Androids can fill a role as a consumer, something people can't do efficiently anymore. Once they're established, however—"

He stopped, punched at his thigh. "Damn!"

"What?"

"Listen, Jessica," Parric said earnestly. "I'm not a

brain or a computer or even a specially educated man. I got picked for this because I was a nobody who could tell when others were nobodies too. Like these androids. What I mean is, it just now hit me what you're here for.'' He waited for confirmation, but she refused to speak, watching him instead as if the *Alpha* itself were dependent upon his next words. ''This program that you and whatshisname, Ike, are making. It's to show the people what they're getting, what they're going to have alongside them, isn't it?''

''Clever,'' she said, without the malice he expected. ''That's right. Ike is the best propagandist trivitographer in the business. He can't stand the thought of them not being human, but he's not so far gone that he can't see the value of what's being tried here.''

''Tried?'' Parric was surprised.

''Well, maybe that was the wrong word, but let's face it, Frank, there's no absolute assurance it's going to work. I told you once I was a little afraid of them myself. And so, I think, are you. Which,'' she added in time to cut him off, ''makes you a rather special person, no matter what you say. I mean, you don't necessarily like this business, but you're doing it because you care about the future, like me.''

''Unfortunately,'' Parric said, deciding she might as well get to know him as well as his charges, ''I don't care all that much about futures and things. I have enough trouble looking out for my own, such as it is.''

''Then why are you so interested in the *Alpha*?''

Ike walked past them, waving, and Parric lifted a perfunctory hand in return. The two small Kellers were trailing behind the cameraman, shotgunning questions he seemed eager to answer as he pointed to his rig, pulled at switches and sliding panels. Parric wondered when he would bring himself up short in the realization that what he was talking to was not human; then dismissed the thought and replaced it with the *Alpha*, a starship launched from the tiny lunar base where ten-score gazers saw things the mundane Earth could not, or would not. Despite his insistence on remaining loyal only to himself, Parric had begun dreaming about the *Alpha* and the ramifications of its promises of something better than stumbling blindly around in a dark full of stars. There were no phrases, no speeches, no manner at all of semantic manipulation that could convey to the woman at his side in an unreal community why the few hopes he had left were sailing through near vacuum toward things he would never comprehend nor live to see.

What it was, then, peeled off in painful layers: "I just am."

And she nodded, while he silently questioned.

But as he turned to seek some answers, a call roused him and he stood to face Mrs. Keller, who was running surprisingly agilely across the street. Afterward, he remembered the oddity, but at the moment he was more interested in what she was saying.

"Doctor! Doctor Parric! Have you heard? Lord, Doctor Parric, there's a war!"

Chapter 3

Parric was on his feet and sidestepping to avoid a collision with the android matron. As his hands snatched at the railing to maintain his balance, he noticed how accurate her reactions were: the quivering lips, slightly moist and confused eyes, the head that twisted in bewildered anguish from his face to Jessica's.

"I heard it. It's a war," Mrs. Keller said as one hand crumpled the drably printed cloth that enveloped her bosom.

"Don't they have a link?" Jessica asked.

"No," he said as he smiled at Mrs. Keller to calm her down. "None in the Towns do. Subvocal communication didn't seem fitting for those who have to pass."

"What are you talking about, doctor?" Mrs. Keller said, her fear shifting through to anger.

"Nothing," Jessica said. "He's being himself again."

And Parric glared before turning away.

"All right, Mrs. Keller, you start from the beginning and tell me what you thought you heard."

"Doctor, you know full well I don't imagine I hear things."

True enough, he thought. Nobody had yet managed to transfer that particular weakness from man.

"Me and Buddy—that's my husband, Miss Windsor—we were listening to the audio because certain people we know haven't been around to fix our trivid, and there was a newsflash that there was a war. I'm telling you, I heard it."

Just as Parric was about to plumb for further details, Ike scurried up the walk. "Brother Parric, you got troubles."

"Great," he said. "If it's a war, Mrs. Keller just told me."

"More than that. You'd better head for the inside." And he was past them into the house before either Parric or Jessica could stop him. Parric did notice, however, that his face was not much less whiter than his hair.

"Mrs. Keller, you'd better go on back home now. I'll call the Central and see what more I can find out. Don't worry about a thing. This isn't the first time there's been a war this century, you know."

"Well, don't I know it," she said, suddenly huffed.

"Nice touch," he muttered to Jessica, who immediately left to join her assistant.

Mrs. Keller sputtered a few more nothings, then turned away to run back across the street. Parric watched, puzzled at something he could not identify, before hurrying inside where the two reporters were sitting in the living room.

There were enough armchairs in the room to accommodate a committee, something Parric had insisted upon when, in choosing furnishings, he had reminded himself of the barren sterility of his own, now nearly forgotten apartment. Set into the wall that faced the front brace of windows was a meter-square screen presently coded to one of the news channels. What he saw as his eyes adjusted to the glare in the dimly lighted room were maps of Eurecom and the New United Kingdom unevenly blotched with a producer's idea of dangerous red. As he sat in the one chair he used most often and waited for it to squirm to his posture, the screen flickered and a sprawling chart of the Eastern Panasian Union and the Japanese Empire faded into view. It, too, was smeared, almost totally covered with the red that now seemed to acquire more a character than the spectrum's segment it represented.

"What—"

And Jessica hushed him over the commentator's return.

"This," said the theatrically somber voice, "shows the latest results from the Panasian block; as much, that is, as we can ascertain considering the clamp on Japan's satellite news network. As of now, no one seems to know who started the war, and no one is admitting it, but Continental Government sources agree that the territory between Eurecom and Western Panasia was definitely the focal point of the attack which, they further estimate, commenced some four weeks ago."

"What's he talking about? How can a war go on for four weeks without anyone knowing about it?"

"Shut up, doctor," Ike said and turned up the volume.

". . . unleashed through self-destruct missiles not

seen since the early days of the last century. Though spotty at best, much was apparently highly contagious and spread through the usual economic intercourse and tourism that regularly occurs between these sectors. There is no indication of how exacting the human damage is, nor what it will be despite the massive aid being rushed to the populations involved. However, it is generally supposed by unnamed sources that fully two million or more have already been fatally afflicted, and there is no doubt that this horrifying, though unofficial, figure will rise.

"I repeat, by ContiGov decree, all Noram citizens will report to their assigned medical centers for inoculations as soon as they have been issued passes by the proper authorities. Should signs of vomiting, nervous spasms, high fever and/or small swellings along the inside of the armpits and side of the neck appear, do not attempt to administer first aid of any kind. Evacuate the premises and report the occurrence immediately to the police.

"It is suggested that all comunits remain tuned to this station for further information and instructions. There will be, repeat, there will be no entertainment programs for the duration of this emergency.

"And now, repeating our previous bulletins—"

Ike stood and slapped the screen into gray, walked to the window, and looked out across the darkened street.

Jessica remained still, taut, as Parric watched her gripping clawlike the arms of her chair. She's been through this before, he thought without knowing why, and he made no move to comfort her.

War, and he was not surprised.

Biological, and he was appalled by that hell.

Inevitable, and that frightened him.

31

"Jess, we'd better leave right away," Ike said, lacking complete conviction.

"No way to get where you'd want to go," Parric said when it was evident Jessica wasn't going to respond. "Not unless someone sends back the vehicle that flew you in. You'd never get your equipment over these hills. No roads, remember?"

"Brilliant," Ike said. "That's just perfect."

"Floyd," Jessica said suddenly. "We'd better get in touch with Floyd."

A lifeline: and the generally granite composure of Coates' manner was sought as balm for their slow comprehension of a new definition of horror. Parric fumbled at the comunit's board for a moment before he was able to code in the private number he had been given for emergencies. None of the three doubted, unvoiced, that their own country hadn't been affected, but they waited childlike for Coates to tell them otherwise.

When the signal cleared and Coates peered into the room, their nightmares were given foundation.

He appeared shaken but still confident though a pressure tic made it seem as if he were winking at them.

"All of you there?"

Parric nodded, then waited until Ike and Jessica moved into range of the screen's sensors.

"What happened, Floyd?" he said, floating above the unperturbed sound of his voice like an observer unattached to the world spinning death. "What do we do?"

"Well, at least you're not hysterical," Coates said.

"Give me a minute," Ike said, "and I'll fix you up."

"You talk too much, Lupozny," Coates said, his face too large to allow Parric to see where he was though he suspected he would not recognize the place could he examine it.

"Give, Floyd," Jessica said, her voice curiously soft, "what do we do?"

"Nothing right now. You've heard the news, so I assume you know some idiot has blown the world apart with some kind of passing plague. Make that plural. Some were too heavy to be carried by the wind, but at least one was portable enough to spread over a hell of a lot of space."

"Us?" Parric said, his face dull in resignation.

"Some of it," Coates admitted after an uncomfortable pause. "Luckily, synthidotes are popping up all over the place, but you'll pardon me if I suspect the speed at which those formulae were handed over. I wouldn't be surprised if those donors were in for a lot of trouble when this is over. Anyway, that's beside the point right now. Some jackass, you see, broadcast the full and unholy details before we could get a clamp down, and now there are panics I haven't seen since the early days of the Ghetto War. Frankie, it was a lot easier at Everlasting, believe me. These people here are tripping all over themselves. I wish I could tell you all more, but I can't."

"Can't, or won't?" Parric said before Jessica could stop him, but Coates ignored him.

"Listen," Coates said, leaning closer, "you'll all have to stay there for the time being. As far as I can tell, it won't be for very long. Just keep the channel open. In case." He glanced to one side, nodded, and looked back. "Frankie, watch out for those children of mine. I wouldn't want them getting hurt.''

And he was gone, fading into a starpoint before Parric could snap back.

Silence, then, that cloaked in ritual fashion the fear and accentuated the relief. Only minor outbreaks. *They would not die.* Riots. *They will not die.*

Ike pushed aside his armchair and began experimenting with the barcab, trying to circumvent the preset liquors that barely had time to settle in a glass before they sheathed his throat. He offered one first to Jessica, who refused, and then to Parric, who took the glass, emptied it, and handed it back for another. Ike nodded in surprise, but Parric would not stay with him, walking instead to the front door.

"Join me?" he asked no one in particular and stepped outside without hearing an answer.

The street was deserted, lights glaring like lanterns across the cityless black night. He looked up and out from under the overhang of the porch roof and stared at the stars slightly blurred by the barrier that closed him out, protected him in. He pushed, probing, grasping with what he had for something he could not have. *Alpha* could not hear him when he whispered, "They've done it. Oh, my God, they've done it.''

Wrenching from a place he had not known was so deep within him, a sob shattered the still evening and there was a coolness and warmth on his cheeks that he wiped away quickly in unreasoning shame.

On alternate blocks streetlamps popped on to complement the charade.

"You know, there've been times when I've forgotten you're really human," Jessica said quietly. Then, "I'm sorry. I've known you less than a day and I had to say that of all things. I'm sorry.''

Though knowing he should have been angered, he could only lift a weak hand in silent absolution.

"You said you were married once."

She said nothing, clucked her tongue as if to dismiss it.

"Contract, was it, or were you a lifer?"

"Lifer," she said after they'd listened to a glass break inside, and another. "He gets violent when he's depressed."

"Nice guy."

"He died. My husband, that is. During the Arabian Wars."

"I . . . I missed it," he said in an odd, token apology. "Too young, they said."

"So was he, but he wanted a ribbon."

Motionless, then, they danced around each other's sorrow without scaling the walls that separated them. In silence.

Lights, like torches thrust into caverns, glared from the lower floors of most of the houses along the street. A door slammed, and another. Parric shuddered away the tension that had cocooned him and watched as old man Dix shambled across the road away from him. Invisible, visible, he moved from black to the serrated pools of streetlamp glow.

Now where? Parric took a step down, remembered Jessica, and asked if she wanted to go with him.

"Where?"

"Funny," he said. "I was just asking myself that same thing. A walk, I guess, to see how the children are doing with this their first real crisis."

"I don't know. No. I think I'll stick around and wait for Floyd to call back."

"If he does, that is," Parric said, walking away. "I

wouldn't stay up all night if I were you. It's not like we were in the middle of all that red, you know.''

"You really don't care all that much, do you?''

He didn't answer, less interested in himself than he was in the sight of Dix skipping from curb to curb. What he didn't need now, he thought as he lengthened his stride, was a senile android without any replacement parts.

He caught up two blocks from the clinic and leaned against a tree while Dix, the lenses of his glasses shining, sat down in the center of the road and began humming to himself.

"You all right, Mr. Dix?'' Parric said, not leaving his spot. There was one thing that had been dunned into him a thousand times during his orientation, and it was simply that an android, when programming skittered, could be uncomfortably strong and unpredictable. The odds of that happening, he had also been told, were infinitesimally small.

"Just passing time, doc,'' the old one said. "Passing the time and looking at the moon. Nice day, isn't it?''

"Sure is,'' Parric said. "A little chilly, though. Don't you think you ought to get inside before you come down with something?''

"A man my age doesn't have to worry about those things, youngster. I'm going to die sooner or later, and it might as well be now as then.''

"Bad attitude,'' Parric said, deciding Dix was harmless and stepping down off the curb. "You're needed, you know.''

"By whom?''

"By me, for one. Who would I fight with if you get away from me?''

"Then why are you always talking about sending me to that McLeod fella somewhere over the hill?"

"Because you're impossible."

Dix rocked slowly, began humming again, and did not protest when Parric took hold of an arm and lifted. Cautiously. Unlimbering, like a balloon filling, Dix stood, swaying until his balance returned. They walked, slowly, until they reached Dix's house and Parric bade him goodnight.

"Sorry for the trouble, doc."

"Forget it," Parric said. "That's what I'm here for, remember?"

Watching as the front door closed and the light was shut off, Parric discovered he was cutting into his palms with his nails, and his upper arms were shaking. Carefully measuring his tread, he blew out a deep breath and decided to deactivate the old man as soon as he could get him to the clinic. There was something seriously wrong within the system that he could not figure out, and he was not about to let the android stick around long enough to become murderous.

Meanwhile, there was the war to worry about.

Brother, he thought, it's going to be a hell of a day.

"Doctor!"

This time he was prepared when Mrs. Keller raced toward him. He held out his hands and caught her by her shoulders, grasping them and spinning around until her energy was spent.

"Now what?"

"Is that any way to talk to a patient, Doctor Parric? I'm in trouble and I need your assistance."

Code. Parric immediately guided her to the nearest light and stared into her face, looking for the telltale squint that indicated a lens malfunction, the one positive sign of a deeper disturbance. Oddly, there was nothing, but she continued to repeat the encoded call for help.

"Mrs. Keller, there doesn't seem to be anything seriously wrong, but perhaps we ought to go to the clinic."

After she readily agreed, he checked his pocket to see if he still had the key, then hurried to the office, tore back her dress, and opened the skin. The diagunit had already proceeded with the cursory, daily check when he rerouted to comprehensive and listened as the android recited the minutely detailed report of what it had done during the day. Except for an unaccountable stammering and a half dozen breaks in the narrative for the emergency signal, he could tell nothing, and after glancing through the test results before sending them to the Central, was still ignorant of her condition.

"I don't get it, Mrs. Keller. Nothing at all seems to be the matter with you."

"That's strange," she said, straightening her clothes. "I feel just fine."

Parric only looked at her.

"But thanks anyway. I hope you're feeling better," she said, and left him standing in the office, the diagunit patiently waiting behind him.

"Yes," he said finally, "I definitely need a vacation."

Outside, he saw Ike striding toward him, leaning forward as if combating a hurricane wind.

"Coates wants you," Ike said, grabbing his arm and tugging. "He won't say why, but when he takes those damned glasses off, he's either planning to fire you or run you for President."

True enough, Parric thought, having seen that gesture many times empty a desk at Everlasting, but he had the feeling that his previous life as a nobody in a nothing business was not the type of material Lupozny was searching for in his preparation of the android documentary.

And in the living room he saw Jessica step quickly back from the screen, and Coates nervously rubbing his glasses against his chest.

"About time," the supervisor said. "You always run off like that in the middle of the night?"

"Trouble," Parric said, expecting the matter to drop, surprised to see Coates replace his eyepieces and stare.

"What kind? Those androids?"

"You win," Parric said, looking to the others for explanations and receiving only shrugs in return. Carefully, then, he explained what had happened to Mrs. Keller and Dix.

"Thought as much," Coates said brusquely. "Now listen carefully because there's no time for questions. Pretty soon now I'll be leaving for another office. I doubt very much that I'll be talking to you again; at least not soon. There's been a spillover from that damnable war on both our coasts. It's bad and getting worse. We don't expect casualties to climb as high as the immediate war zones, but we've got massive panic on our hands in most urban areas and the most important thing right now is to try to regain some sane stability. That won't be easy, nor will it happen soon."

"We'll pack," Ike said.

"Don't bother. You're staying right where you are. The dangerous infection period is something less than forty-eight hours—though that's plenty long enough for efficiency—and your particular area should be brushed by the plague winds in less than . . . damn it, you should have been told before! The winds should have passed over you just after 2400 yesterday. Since you're all still alive and show no symptoms, I'm assuming the Town's protection at least spared you that unpleasantness. I wish I could say the same for the others.''

''McLeod!'' Parric said, unable to refrain from interrupting.

''Relax. At last word he was fine. Some of the others, however, lost their pin-sized heads and ran off. Which brings us to our children.''

Parric groped behind him and sat on the arm of a chair already occupied by Jessica. She touched him once, left him alone, and Coates took time out to smile.

''Nice,'' he said. ''At least you're friends.''

''Not exactly,'' Jessica said. ''But we get along. You might say we understand each other.''

''I thought you would.''

''Meaning?'' Parric said.

''Forget it for now. I haven't much time. Wait a minute . . .'' and the screen blanked as Coates' face disappeared. There seemed to be a partition of sorts blocking a clear view of the room the supervisor was in, and the implication did not settle well in Parric's already protesting nerve centers. Ike, meanwhile, had run into the back room and had returned with several cases of recorders which he arranged in a semicircle in front of the wall.

''Blackmail?'' Parric said.

''History,'' Ike snapped. ''You gotta have faith, brother Parric.''

''Forget it,'' Jessica said. ''You're talking to the—''

40

"Okay," Coates said, reappearing, this time wearing a bulky outergarment. "Time's almost up. You're the last Town to know so listen and learn. The Town's barriers are not completely plague preventative. They can't be or you wouldn't have any air to breathe at all. What it boils down to is that one strain of this plague can have an effect on the androids' biomechanism filaments. Frankie, you've already seen what it can do, generally nothing more than a temporary upset. There have been reported cases, however, when the androids get downright nasty. Obviously, the human synthidotes are useless here, but we're working on that as fast as we can. Which, I know, doesn't do you a hell of a lot of good, but it's all we've got at the moment. You have to be careful, Frank. You are ordered to deactivate as many of them as you can before the night is over. Don't take chances, of course, but try not to abandon the Town for another twenty-four hours, should that move become necessary. Your biggest problems will most likely come from the outlying towns still functioning with human populations."

"Why?" Jessica asked unnecessarily.

"You insist on interrupting me."

"My prerogative," she said.

"Would you mind?" Parric said, his annoyance carrying him to his feet as if getting closer to Coates' image would allow him to hear better.

"Thank you, Frank," Coates said. "Simply, Jess, the smaller towns have taken advantage of the situation, and not surprisingly either. Local small fry have made themselves big, that sort of thing. They've also been fed a lot of half-truths through the trivid about the Towns. Don't," he said, louder, "tell me the project was supposed to be a big dark secret. You know it, I know it, but a Cabinet member, rest his plague-pocked soul, decided it wasn't worth the bother with the world going to hell. Now there are a lot of people who believe you've been testing these strains and have accidentally let them loose. Neither you nor the children are very popular.''

"Fools,'' Parric said.

"You're interrupting,'' Jessica said.

"No matter,'' Coates said, "I have to go now.''

Instantly, the three were arrayed in front of the comunit. But there was nothing they could say. Coates surveyed them, nodded a rueful smile, and his hand grew as he reached out to break the connection. Parric was the first at the barcab.

"Anyone want to listen to the news?'' Jessica said.

"Forget it,'' Ike said as he collected his equipment.

"No need right now,'' Parric agreed. "We know all we have to. What we've got to do is stay put until we're told otherwise. Obviously, Floyd places high values on this Town.''

Jessica worried at her hair, then crossed the room and pulled an armless lounge in front of the windows. She pushed at the cushioned curves top and bottom, then stretched out, slapping at its sides until she realized it was static.

"You frightened?'' Parric said.

"Her?'' Ike's hand grabbed an offered glass as he returned from the back room. "Listen, doc, we've been in riots from Fairbanks to Managua, and she hasn't lost a hair once. Whenever the ContiGuard has to move in somewhere, she's usually right behind the first man. She has this compulsion about suicide, you see. I just wish she'd leave me out of it.''

"How real are they?'' she asked, pointing out the

window before closing her eyes and folding her hands beneath her head.

Parric watched her settling, unwillingly comparing her finely soft features to his own distorted ones: a nose too large, a chin too small, eyes that burrowed away from the world beneath brows that were thick and overhanging. He blinked and caught Ike smiling, watching him as he unconsciously traced a finger along the short road of his jaw. The photographer must have seen this reaction to his partner in a hundred men, and the thought made Parric angry.

"Real enough," he said when she repeated her question. "They have the same outward emotional responses and reactions that we do, though the popular notion of a continuously running recording tape is totally erroneous. There is, if I understand it correctly, a patch of filaments with microdotted impulse centers connected to the android's so-called brain which interreact in such a way as to make near perfect charlatans of them. It's those filament brushes that Floyd is worried about. Partly metallic, partially a synthetic cellular structure, they're ordinarily immune to diseases of our flesh."

"Ordinarily," Ike said sourly.

"Their only fault, that I've been able to see, is that because they're also delicate mechanisms, their physical reactions are slightly faster than ours, to protect them from getting badly damaged. Normal falls, as I told you before, are one thing, but if you sneak up on one and club him over the head as hard as you can, this time he won't go down. Unless, that is, he's been programmed otherwise, which most of the ones we're using haven't been."

"Well, why not?"

"Protection, m'dear," Ike said with a look to Parric. "Clout a man over the head and you'll usually bash in a fair chunk of his skull. Do the same to one of these . . . things, and he has to know he's in danger in order to protect himself."

"Right," Parric said. "If an android drops to the ground because he's been attacked, the odds are he'll be hit again, and maybe destroyed."

"But why?"

"Because, for one thing, androids don't bleed. And if he doesn't bleed, the attacker thinks he hasn't done the job properly, and he strikes again. And if he sees that what he has is an android, he'll make damned sure he does it right. This is all hypothetical, of course, and statistically improbable, but you can be sure that if you hit an android hard enough he'll protect himself just as hard, and believe me, he can do a fine job on a man's arm."

"Ask a simple question, I get a lecture," Jessica said.

"He's programmed that way," Ike said, laughing until he realized Parric had not taken the joke well. "Sorry," he said, but his grin remained long enough to prove he hadn't meant it.

"I've got to get to the clinic," Parric said suddenly. "Anyone want to go with me?"

"Kind of late, isn't it, doc?" Ike said.

"You have a short memory," Jessica said as she uncoiled from the lounge to follow Parric. "Those sweet little children of Floyd's have to be put to sleep."

"Tuck them in for me," Ike said, making himself comfortable on the floor near the barcab. "I've changed my mind. I want to keep an eye on the news in case something comes up we should know about."

"What's to know?" Parric said. "We're not going anywhere."

"Then call it professional courtesy to my fellow reporters out there who are getting all the scoops and bonuses while I'm stuck in a damned town without a damned human in it who can get drunk decently."

As they left the house, Parric looked back to see the screen fill with a picture of a hospital ward. He closed the door quickly, feeling the skin at his side begin to itch and perspiration bead across his forehead.

Chapter 4

He walked rapidly until Jessica, who was trying to keep up with him without running, took him by the arm to check his rush. As they passed under a streetlamp, he saw the shadows the artificial light swept briefly across her face and, though she avoided a direct glance, the trails of lingering wisps of fear. It puzzled him that she had managed to cover all those riots without breaking, but a solution came to him before he could block it: riots were people, and even in mobs they could be somewhat predictable; androids on the verge of collapse could not.

The itching at his side persisted. Resisting the impulse to stop, yank out his shirt, and look, he told himself it was merely a sympathetic reaction to the scenes of the already inflicted he had spotted before leaving the house. His Town had been fortunate, as many others would be; but many would not escape, had not done so. He thought of the cities and an unbidden image of a loathsome, bloated Coates popped and vanished, and he began to run.

At the clinic he dumped all the patients' records onto

the desk while Jessica, unordered, rolled out the diagunit.

"Here," he said, handing her a small pad. "These are the numbers of the occupied homes. Call them and get them here so they arrive one family at a time." He brushed aside space for her near the comunit and showed her where the cards were to be inserted. "When they answer," he said, "Say *Doctor Parric requires you*, then read off the names. Forget those numbers there; they're only computer identification. These androids aren't coded to respond to them anymore."

"Sounds like fun."

Parric could not help a startled glare, but she smiled quickly and began before he could say anything.

"What happens," she said after completing the first call, "when we cut them off?"

He stopped his nervous fussing around the diagunit and looked around the small room. "Damn, I hadn't thought of that."

"If there's the slightest thing wrong, they might not react the way they're supposed to if they see a bunch of shells propped up against the walls."

"Nothing to it," he said. He unlocked the back door, poked his head out, and nodded. "We'll put them out here. In one door and out the other."

"Very efficient," she said.

"What do you have against me, Miss Windsor?" he said as he fell into a pacing wait.

"Not a thing," she said, one hand poised with the second family's code. "I'd like to know what it is that you have against us?"

"Us?"

"People."

"Nothing," he said shortly. "Not a thing one way or the other."

Immediately he finished speaking, the Bonettos walked in, Dan in the lead, followed by his wife, Marion, and one child. Parric greeted them warmly and told them to prepare for examination.

"What's the trouble, doc?" Dan said. "It's the middle of the night."

"Nothing serious," Parric assured him as he turned the three around and took out his scapel. "Just something new from the Central. You know them by now. Once they get an itch, nothing short of . . . short of an earthquake can stop them from scratching."

"Seems funny, what with a war going on and everything. I'd like to know what they're doing, getting us . . . up . . . like—"

The android slumped, was imitated by Marion and the child. Jessica did not wait to make the second call, and Parric dragged the lifeless husks into the backyard. When he returned, she was preparing her third summons.

"Damn things are heavy," he said, wiping his hands against his thighs. "They must weigh a ton, at least."

"Out of shape, clerk," she said, grinning, but Parric resented the reference to a time he had been trying to file in an inactive drawer. It was bad enough that his Town, his world, was fast shifting out from under him without her reminder of what he would have to return to when it was over.

Slowly, the inhabitants arrived, were deactivated and placed on the outside where they couldn't be seen. Almost half of them had been taken care of without incident when Jessica frowned and looked up. "Funny," she said. "He hung up on me."

"Who?"

"That old man. Dix, right?"

Parric nodded. "Damn, even in a crisis he can't be civil. Well, I already know there's something wrong with that one." And he told her what had happened earlier.

"I saw you walk him back to the house. He looked all right to me."

"He wasn't," said Parric, "believe me. But we'll have to get him later."

It was past midnight before they had completed the list and he had returned the diagunit to its cubicle. He was tired, and a glance outside before leaving almost unnerved him. There were shadows cast in gray moonlight in varying attitudes of standing and sitting; statuary in grotesque poses of unnatural death, waiting without conception of patience for a spark of resurrection. He looked down at Bonetto's child and passed a hand over its head, his palm tingling against the finely woven hair. Through the rapidity of the simple operations he had not been able to do much more than think about the next one, but now he felt as if he had killed, however temporarily, the only things in his life that had needed him. And, in thinking, he told himself sternly that they were only androids, mechanical dolls, fancified robots, experiments in a complicated scheme to sustain life until a planet learned to live it properly; telling, but not believing.

Jessica stood quietly next to him as he arranged a jacket tighter around the chest of a man.

"The others, Frank," she said, and stood aside when he reentered the clinic, folded the smock, and draped it carefully over the back of his chair.

"You wonder why I haven't been more than a

49

clerk," he said bitterly, and pointed toward the rear wall. "Out there is why. One step forward, twenty back."

"The others," she repeated. "They didn't come in."

"How many?" Almost as if he did not care.

"Eight."

He clasped his hands, brought them up to his chin, and gently tapped the bone that had done little but enable him to form the words that passed each of his days. "Who?" he asked.

She shuffled through the cards she still held in her hand, but continued to watch him carefully as if expecting him to collapse as his children had done. "Dix," she said finally, "Mrs. Keller and her children, the Warners, Dorski, and Fabor."

"Okay," he said, "let's get them down here as best we can."

"For a moment there I thought you were going to let them go," she said, following him through the reception room to the outside.

"For a moment there I was," he said, smiling. "I get depressed easily, you see."

"So I noticed," she said.

"Tell me something," he said as they stepped off the walk into the street. "Just who are you? There are at least a dozen Towns, maybe even more, but why did you have to come to me?"

"Chance," she said, "and Fate. The will of the gods. The spin of the wheel. The track of the stars."

He laughed and tucked his hand between her arm and side. "You think I believe that? Floyd must have had something up his sleeve. He never does anything without a purpose."

"He worries about me."

"Why? Are you a vital in the field?"

"In his, I am, I guess. There's . . . what's that?"

She pointed, he reluctantly took his eyes from her face and stared. Halfway to where Ike was presumably depleting the barcab supplies was a dark-figured milling, shapes that blurred together, then split apart into segments of formless writhing. Without thinking, Parric quickened his step, Jessica trailing. Closer, and he saw the androids who had not answered his summons. They were dancing in a Stygian parody of a reel. Almost at once he became aware of a softly intense humming, a wordless Gregorian chant that drifted out of the dark shapes to lift into the canopy of branches that capped them.

Soft, loud, stretching to a high-pitched whine bordering on a scream, dropping to caverns of rumbling like a stampede of mammoths to oblivion.

Parric rubbed at one cheek with a trembling knuckle while Jessica leaned against his arm, her hands grasping tightly.

"Mad," he whispered, but it was too loud and a figure broke from the demented circle and rushed toward them, followed by the others still chanting.

"Do you like my song?" Dix said.

"Do you like my dance?" Mrs. Keller said.

"Join us," said the Warners, their youthfully molded faces wide-eyed, their mouths open with lips unmoving.

Jessica uttered what might have become a scream, but she was tugged away from Parric and whirled into the arms of a man and a boy who used her for a pivot in a laughing London Bridge. Parric tried to reach her but Mrs. Keller and a broad-armed Fabor each took

51

one of his hands and led him away in an evergrowing snake dance that soon converged upon itself to form a ragged circle. He struggled, but their grips were too strong. His fingers already ached under the constant pressure.

"Sing," Dix said, laughing and squatting to make himself the hub of the wheel, rocking in time to the slaps of their feet.

"The doctor is too quiet," Dorski said when he and Mrs. Keller's son returned with Jessica. "He needs to relax."

"A lovely day, isn't it, Miss Windsor?" Mrs. Keller said.

"Too warm," Mrs. Warner said, pulling at her clothes.

"Never. It is getting a bit chilly, don't you think?" Mr. Fabor said, pulling sharply on Parric's arm.

Jessica tried smiling when Dix lightly commanded her, but she turned to Parric, who was squirming one hand far too slowly from Mrs. Keller's grip. He kept telling himself, under the tow of magnetic fear, to play the game because they were still quite harmless, but the words wouldn't come to Jessica, and he croaked when he should have laughed.

"The doctor must be tired after a hard day's work," Dix said, still on the ground. "Maybe we should let him go."

Around again, shuffling into a trot in a counterclockwise ring.

"The sun isn't as bright as it used to be," Mrs. Warner said. "Perhaps I'm tired and should be in bed."

Parric tried to see her through the darkness, the lights barely giving her face a form. "Maybe," he said, gasping at a lanced needle that settled in his wrist, "you should see me at the clinic. You might not be well."

"Yes," said Jessica, to Parric's relief. "You could be getting sick. There's something going around, you know."

"My children are fine," Mrs. Keller said, "but I think it's a bit too warm."

"The doctor still looks tired. Do you like my song?"

"Indeed, and immensely so," Mr. Fabor said and broke the now running circle to shake Dix's hand. Parric instantly shook his other hand free and ran to Jessica, who had been released and was swaying. Grabbing her by the waist, he tried to run her back to the house, but she was too dizzy and he forced himself to walk.

"Fine song," Fabor said, and began humming again.

"Warm," Mrs. Keller said, "but I like it that way."

"Where's the doctor?"

Parric heard, knew Jessica had by her gasp, and he ducked onto the sidewalk, using the lawns to escape the light.

"Singing," a child's voice said faintly.

"Fine idea. Why don't we all?"

Parric looked over his shoulder as the eight simulacra rejoined hands and continued their surging hymn. They were directly in the pale light, and had he not been aware of what they were, he would have thought them drunkards escaped from a midsummer's party.

By the time they had reached the porch, he and Jessica had separated quickly, having been made abruptly aware of their contact when Ike called out and asked if they were all right.

"What's going on?" he demanded as they hurried

past him into the living room. "I thought you were going to cut them off or something. Those things are ruining my appetite. Are they nuts?"

"It could be worse," Jessica said, slumping onto the backless lounge, holding her head while her hair curtained her face. "They could hate us, you know."

Ike poked aside a drape and watched, shaking his head and chuckling every few seconds at an unseen antic. Parric, emptying a glass, noticed that while the trivid was still on, the volume had been reduced to a whisper. When he tried to raise it back to normal, nothing happened.

"Fix the picture," Jessica said.

Parric looked again and realized the extradimentional qualities of the comunit had left the screen, giving it a curiously flat look.

"Transmission," Ike said without turning away from the street scene. "It started a while ago. Weak, I think. I don't know."

Whatever the reason, Parric didn't think it made much difference. Even without the proper sound, he could see clearly that the situation was unrelentingly bad, perhaps, as Coates had said before signing off, getting worse. The news network had, sometime while he was gone, abandoned its more horrifying glimpses of the plague, concentrated now on lines of solemn people waiting dully for immunization; helicopters and hovercats were flying low over apparently unaffected or already treated streets and small towns outside the cities, local and Continental politicians visiting those in the lines, smiling as they graciously accepted their own inoculations without wincing, holding the hands of children calm and oddly shy about having their pictures taken. Solidarity and stolid acceptance was the impression, and Parric had to admire the way the media were obviously working overtime to calm what panic there was.

"Used to do that kind of thing myself," Ike said, sitting next to him on the floor. His face had regained its rougelike contrast to his white hair, but his eyes were developing puffs of dark and they blinked too much, making Parric nervous. "Sit in a dark room and watch the reels sweep by. Clip and nip here, snatch and discard there, and that's what you have: shoulder to shoulder in the midst of adversity. Nicely done."

"A good thing, though, at a time like this."

Ike scratched at his neck, pushed with one finger at the wad of gum punching out his cheek. "Maybe. I just hope they don't get used to it. Like that singing or whatever it is out there. A guy could get used to it if he tried."

Parric was tempted to tell him to go out and join the android revel if he felt that way, but stopped himself. Ike had meant nothing by it, was only trying to make the best of what was an extremely uncertain situation. And the more he watched the screen, the more he thought things might not be so bad after all, that probably Coates had been characteristically exaggerating and it wouldn't be all that long before he sent out the order to reinstate the Town's daily life. He felt himself lulled, comforted by the sights distorted before him, and he ignored the comments Lupozny was making concerning the technical inadequacies of the filming. He didn't care that someone had left one scene on too long, another cut off too quickly; what he wanted now was to sleep and awaken in the morning to find Jessica, Ike, and all their equipment gone, and the androids people again, complaining about the weather and wondering when they could send their children to school.

His head nodded toward his upraised knees, but he jerked awake when Jessica screamed.

Ike had already gotten to his feet and was standing with his arms around her shoulders when Parric finally shook off the hypnotic stupor. Jessica's reserve had at last vanished, and Ike was not far behind her.

There was a face in the window, eerily twisted in a mirthless smile. After the second needed for recognition, Parric rushed to the door and went out.

"Willard," he said, his throat closed near to a strangle by anger, "what the hell do you think you're doing?"

The street was quiet, but Parric didn't take the time to look for the others. The old man was moving awkwardly along the meter-wide porch as if he had sprained one ankle but was determined to walk on it despite the pain. His hands reached out, palms up, then dropped to his side.

"I was just looking for another party, doc. Can't sleep with all that racket going on, you know. Damned people ought to be more considerate of others. Us old folks need our sleep, you know, but there ain't many who give a damn."

Relieved that Dix seemed to be back to his usual self, Parric took him by the arm and led him to the sidewalk. "Tell you what," he said. "You go on home and I'll make a few calls. I don't think they'll disturb you anymore."

"Can't sing worth a damn, you know."

Parric shrugged.

"Well, you're all right, doc, you know that? Nice to have you around."

"Whatever you say, Will. Now beat it before I call

McLeod and have him turn you into a lawnmower."

The old man laughed and hurried away, the limp gone, replaced by a monotonic muttering. Parric backed slowly to his own door, a hand behind him for guidance. Peaceful once and void of menace, the street had suddenly become enveloped in a coarse veil of alien fear, an intruder tinged with madness that hovered, cloaked and content to wait.

"Well?" Ike said, alone in the front room. Parric looked around for Jessica, then followed Ike's nod to the back. "Tired," he explained. "Nerves more than anything."

"I don't blame her," Parric said. "That was Dix. He seems to be normal again, but I wouldn't bet on it now. The way I feel, in fact, I wouldn't bet that this house won't suddenly sprout legs and walk off into some goddamned Arctic lake."

"Listen, brother Parric, do you realize it's going onto three hours past midnight? Maybe we both ought to get some sleep."

Parric dropped into his chair and rubbed his face with both hands. "You go ahead. I just remembered I should make a call."

Ike stared, then shrugged and disappeared into the bedroom without further question. Parric watched as the door slid to, and wondered how long they had been together, how much longer it would take before she recovered enough from a poorly contained grief that had lingered so long to contract with Lupozny. He himself had seldom been attracted to women, and when he had, the frustrations of not receiving deep concern in return had been sufficient to drive him deeper within himself and the work a machine could have done a hundred times faster.

57

"All right, dope, cut it," he told himself, and rose to switch the screen from the trivid circuit to the comunit channels. It would be no use trying to reach Coates or any of the other officials in the agency that employed him; if transmissions across the board were, in fact, weakening, it would be better to try something closer to home. Better, therefore, he thought, to raise Cam and find out if he could how the situation fared throughout the Town complex. It might help him decide what to do in case trouble became too volatile for safety.

It was a full three minutes after he had coded in the sequence before the gray haze shattered and McLeod's barklike face peered into the room. He grinned, his lips moved, but Parric could near nothing.

"Cam," he said finally, "can you hear me okay?"

McLeod nodded, began speaking again.

"Hold it, Cam," Parric said. "There's something wrong with the reception on my end. I can't hear a word you're saying. And if you'll excuse me, you look absolutely rotten."

McLeod scratched his hairless scalp vigorously and cupped a hand in front of his mouth to conceal a yawn. His face sagged as if gravity in his Town had increased and was trying to pull him to the planet's core. He seemed worried but not frightened and despite his muteness, Parric was momentarily reassured.

"Listen," he said after watching McLeod mime a question, "I'm all right, no problem, but I got a couple of reporters, historians, stuck in here with me. Nothing bad yet. I've got most of the place settled except for seven, eight, that I can't get into the clinic. Do you have any trouble with singing androids?"

McLeod laughed and held his forehead as if to say he

58

expected as much from Parric's end. Then he held up a single finger.

"You've got one left?"

McLeod nodded.

"Is it stable?"

McLeod nodded again just as the picture began to waver. Parric slapped at the toggled panel that angled out from the side of the screen, but seconds later the unit went gray.

"Damn," he said and switched back to trivid where the result was the same.

"Great. Now what?"

A yawn answered his question. Though he felt as though he were a captive and should be standing guard for the androids' next series of escapades, his eyes began to sting in sleepy temptation, and it wasn't long after he'd stretched out on the lounge that concern for potential danger was shunted aside by slumber.

Chapter 5

It might have been the metallic clatter of dragging chains, or the chattering of nail teeth. Yet again, the rythmic count of robots' feet as they danced in five-four time across the skeleton of steel-ribbed buildings, a ballet macabre to the tune of women weeping. Motes of suncolor rushed past his eyes as if he were running, congealed into swirling, curling arms of blinding plasma. Spinning. Spinning still faster to create a vortex into which he was carried without moving, accompanied by the chains, the teeth, the steel-like feet. And it was desert warm, baking, preparing to burn when he opened his eyes and found himself on the lounge, his shirt opened at the neck, and the sun, magnified by the glass, working at his skin.

He shook his head sharply and grunted to his feet, wriggling shoulders and back until the throbbing in his muscles faded into the background of the noises from the kitchen.

He looked at his watch and saw it was 0935.

Confound it, he thought as he hurried from the room, why did they let me sleep so late?

Ike was at the ovenwall, pulling from its small mouth steaming silvered platters of a dinnertime meal. He was dressed as he had been and smiled broadly when Parric came in.

"Enjoy, doc," he said, sweeping a hand toward the place already set at the crowded table. "It's a beautiful day and, by God, we're still alive."

Jessica was already seated, had changed into a shirt exactly like Parric's; the billows, however, did little to camouflage her figure, or her youth. Her mouth was full and she didn't speak, but smiled, nodded to the empty chair and began choking. Ike laughed, slapped her on the back, and seated himself.

" Come on, doc," he said. "Will you sit down, for crying out loud?"

"I don't believe it," Parric said when sleep finally made room for annoyance. "You're acting like there's a picnic going on out there. Has anyone thought to check the trivid for news? Did anyone check outside to see if the androids are up and around? Why didn't you get me up? What's—"

"Hold it," Ike said. "Relax an hour or two, will you?"

"But—"

"Frank," Jessica said, leaning back to stare as though distance would give her a sharper focus on his face. "We didn't wake you because we all needed sleep after yesterday. Nobody's a hero around here, you know, and we haven't got the resources to play at being supermen. What's the hurry, anyway?"

"I don't believe it," Parric said, was all he could say.

"Eat," Ike said.

"Later. I'm going down to the clinic to be sure none

of the others have tried fooling around with last night's operations. And," he added before turning away, "one of you might try the comunit and trivid to see if we have any power. It went off last night after . . . after you went to bed. We could be completely cut off for all I know."

Gaining little satisfaction from their astonishment, he nodded once at them and left the house.

It was, as they had said, a beautiful day, but he spent little time grading it against days past. The clinic, as far as he could tell, had been untouched by the previous night's revelry, and when he glanced out the back door he saw the better part of the Town's population exactly as he had left them. He relaxed, then, and leaned against the door, watching the androids, convincing himself that what had happened was not the result of a petrifying nightmare. The simulacra had lost their specter aura, were now nothing more than characterless mannequins waiting to be summoned back into their roles, posing as people in a peopleless community. He laughed at himself, permitted the laugh to show as a crooked smile, and was amazed that he had allowed them to frighten him that much. They were nothings, and they would remain so until he decided otherwise.

"Fine," he said to them. "Don't do anything I wouldn't do."

On the way back to the house, however, his uneasiness returned. Under the open lamp of the sun, the Town seemed normal, but before he had traveled two blocks he knew the malady had not been removed by some magical, all-encompassing nightwitch. There was quiet without motion, silence without birdsong or children's play. The houses could have been shells or plastic façades propped up by the wind. Nothing moved, no one called; porches were deserted and the curtains in the windows remained tightly closed.

He tried, once, clapping his hands, but there was less than an echo.

He stayed on the sidewalk, deliberately coming down hard on his heels to create a racket, a marching call for the androids to live.

He whistled, groping for and sometimes finding the meandering tune that Dix had composed for the insanity ball of the dark morning hours.

He considered knocking on a few doors to see what the response would be. Perhaps Mrs. Keller would invite him in to breakfast, or Dorski would challenge him to four-level chess. Perhaps, he thought, but didn't leave the walk. There was still too much of a chance that he would find nothing but the cracked mirror laugh he had heard during his sleep; that, he decided, would be a bit too much to take so early in the day.

"Hey!"

He looked up from staring at his shoes and saw a figure with a deformed head backing away from him. A blink, and it was Ike with his camera. Parric shook his head, wondering what would make a man react so when the world outside was collapsing in tears.

"History?" he asked.

"You got it," Ike said, taking the unit from his shoulder and resting it against his hip. When Parric caught up with him, he was already scanning the neighborhood for his next shot.

"Why don't you use the little one?" Parric said when Ike again hefted the bulky cylinder to his eye.

"You mean like old Jess carries? I don't know. It does the same things, but . . . a feel, let's say. I don't know."

Parric didn't either, and did not pretend he understood. He left Lupozny walking toward the end of the street nearest the barrier and returned inside where, goaded by Jessica, he ate. Little, but enough to convince himself he was sated and could take in no more.

"No wonder you're skinny," she said, clearing the table. "I checked, and the comunit's still out. Nothing but static. For all we know, we're the last ones alive on the whole planet."

"Don't," Parric said. "That's no way to talk."

"Wouldn't you like it better that way?"

She followed him into the living room, adjusting the strap of a recorder over her shoulder. He turned but she had already moved past him to the trivid wall where she flipped a toggle and pointed. "See?" she said when sufficient time brought them what they were looking for. "Nothing."

"Okay, I believe you," he said, suddenly confused. "I don't get it, Jessica. One minute you're nice and the next you act like I was still at Everlasting and had called in your policy. I don't understand."

"I promised Floyd I'd be nice to you," she said, heading for the door. "Sometimes I forget."

When she had left, he straddled the lounge and watched her progress down the steps and off in the direction Ike had taken. She had pinned a mikedisc to her shirt and her head was slightly inclined as she spoke into it.

Make it good, he thought, and be sure to tell them what it's all about in my mechanical Eden. And while you're at it, be sure to spell my name right. Some people think it's Parrish.

"Damn it," he said, and punched at the lounge's fabric, wincing when his knuckles came away burned.

64

He noticed then the dull red ring around his wrist and, as he cautiously twisted it from side to side, remembered the grip that had vised it.

Listen, Frankie, Coates had told him once, *those little beasties are composed of some of the most delicate machinery the world has ever come across. You should see the ones the whitecoats have working around their labs: four and five eyes, micro- and macroscopic, screw off a hand and plug in a scapel or a laser . . . but let me tell you something, son, those little bastards can tear your head off if they've a mind to. If you're ever in trouble with a maverick, get him where it hurts. Fast.*

Where it hurts, Parric thought. Easier said than done.

Determined to find something, anything, that would reconnect him to any sector of humanity, he returned to the comunit and was ready to take off the protective panel to probe its insides when he heard someone calling him.

"What?" he said, rushing to the porch, thinking the androids had finally turned against them.

"Company." It was Ike, and his camera was gone. "People company."

Parric hesitated a moment, then started to grin until Ike scowled it away.

"Don't get your hopes up, brother. They've brought along some bad presents."

Quickly they moved the two blocks to the edge of the Town. The last house and its yard gave way to an area that had not been totally cleared when the excavations had been made. This patch of unchecked growth continued to the slope of the hill like a dry moat with nothing in its way, but some fifteen meters into it were large rectangular cases bolted onto concrete slats

65

embedded in the ground. Boundaries, air shafts, and the housings for the barrier's minor controls and alarm systems.

Jessica was standing next to one, turning her head only when she heard the men approach, then looking back toward the rise beyond the transparent wall. Parric saw there were a score, perhaps more, of men standing in a ragged line, waiting.

"From Oraton," he said when she could hear his whisper. "It's about seventeen, maybe twenty kilometers from here. Only a couple of renegade hunters have ever come across this place, and not often what with game practically nonexistent. I told them we were testing computerized transsubstantial immortality." He grinned at her confusion. "It doesn't mean a thing, but it sounded good and kept them away." He looked up at their visitors. "At least, I thought it did."

One of the strangers took a step forward, waving. He, like the others, wore a hunter's tight-fitting costume, splotched green and brown in an odd but effective attempt at camouflage.

"You the boss?" the man said, raising his voice to not quite a shout.

"That's you, doc," Ike said when Parric didn't answer.

"I suppose I am," Parric called back, ignoring the jibe. "What do you want?"

"Then your place is the one with the plague."

Parric saw immediately what had happened, what was likely to. The trivid had not retreated to its pacification program rapidly enough for some, and the men from Oraton were going to erradicate what was believed to be a source of death before they were infected. Unless they were already, Parric thought uncomfortably. He debated, then climbed to the top of the casing and lifted a hand to block the glare of the sun.

"Look, there's nothing here for you," he said. "Just me and my friends. We don't have any—"

"Don't tell us what you've got, mister," the man said, glancing back at his friends, who nodded. "We've been watching you for a long time. We know what's going on here. You got andies in there, and you killed them with that plague. I saw their bodies myself. Now we want in so we can clean the place out before it gets to our people." He pointed behind him to several men who were standing alongside containers Parric guessed carried some sort of flammable liquids. He shook his head.

"Sorry," he said. "I can't let you in. I have my orders from the government—"

The man laughed, shortly, more like coughing. "Well, we got our orders, too, mister. You and your people have damn near wrecked this country and we aren't going to let it all happen around here. So why don't you let us in and no one'll get hurt."

Jessica grabbed a handful of Parric's shirt and tugged. He kept his eyes on the shifting men and bent down.

"They can't get in, can they?"

"No, and they know it. You saw it when you came in yourself. The barrier has three sections, a couple of meters apart. Where they are now is as close as they can get. Unless they have a patchkey, which is next to impossible."

"They have guns, though," Ike said.

"I can see that, Lupozny. What I don't understand is how they think they can threaten us. If they shoot us, they can't get in. If they don't, we won't let them in."

"Yeah," Ike said, "but we can't get out."

"Can they shoot through that?" Jessica said.

Parric nodded. "The barrier can absorb some of the energy of whatever they have to throw at us, but not all of it. If they stay where they are and we sit here staring at them—"

"Hey, mister, you going to let us in?"

Parric felt a laugh slide into his throat. He tried, but couldn't stop it and knew he wasn't helping by showing his disdain. Stepping down from the casing, he faked a cough and told Jessica and Ike to head back toward the house, which they did without question.

"Listen," he said as he backed slowly away, "you can't get in and we've enough supplies to last for years. Why don't you just forget it and go on back to Oraton?"

"Mister," the man shouted back, "just don't stick your head outdoors again. We're thinking maybe you don't settle any less easy in our stomachs than those andies." Immediately, he raised his weapon and fired. Parric sprawled onto the ground as a shell fountained earth where he had been standing. Projectiles, he thought, as he got up to run before the crest of their laughter. Small favors. At least they haven't got hold of any lasers.

Using the trees for cover, he darted from bole to bole until he reached the house, then dashed up the walk, his skin feeling as though it were puckering in anticipation of being punctured. By the time he had fumbled with the front door latch and had stumbled inside, he was also feeling more than a little foolish.

"Nice run," Ike said, offering him a drink, shrugging when it was refused.

"It's silly," Parric said, straining to keep from panting in front of Jessica. "They couldn't have reached me, not from there."

"I'd guess they have the Town surrounded," Ike said. "They might have gotten lucky."

"Ike!"

Parric, pleased at Jessica's outburst, suddenly felt his legs' ability to hold him up drain, fill with lead. He quickly dropped into the nearest chair and said, "Now what?"

"What's to worry?" said Lupozny. "We've got enough food for an army. I'll bet there's enough power in that generator to keep the place running practically forever. You said it before: they can't get in unless we let them in. Stalemate. We win."

"Maybe," Jessica said, "but I'm more confused now than ever. Frank, if there's such a horrible plague going around the country, the world, why aren't those men sick?"

"I don't know. You're asking me?"

Ike laughed and waved a glass in their direction. "Listen, what's to worry? They're not, and that's the point. Maybe they're already immunized. Maybe they're naturally immune. Who knows?"

"Maybe," Parric said, "they're sick and don't know it yet." He tried not to sound smug, but Lupozny was getting on his nerves. "I may be dumb, but I'm not all that stupid. Coates said there was a spillover. If that thing has a life of, what did he say, less than forty-eight hours? Well, incubation might be at least that. The androids started acting strange yesterday morning—"

"So long ago," Jessica said quietly, not interrupting.

"—and their insides are a great deal more sensitive than ours. According to Floyd, we're fairly well protected, but if those people out there haven't been attended to, then they're dying on their feet and don't know it.''

There was nothing for Lupozny to say, but his face left little for translation. Even if they had the opportunity to escape, they dared not; infection was still too dangerous a possibility. He grumbled, began complaining that he had left his camera outside, and started making noises about fetching it until Jessica told him to shut up and find a place to sit and count the blades of grass in the lawn.

Parric walked out to the kitchen to escape their bickering. Standing at the slit of a window, he tried peering through the deep and thick undergrowth that carpeted the hill beneath the trees, looking for signs of movement that might betray his . . . what, he wondered, should I call them? Attackers? Not likely, since they could hardly do much damage as long as the barrier remained powered. In a distorted sense, they might be called his guardians, keeping him inside, stifling any temptations he might have had to leave the Town and thus expose himself to the plague.

He chewed on his lower lip, then fisted a hand and scraped his teeth with one knuckle.

What if he were wrong in estimating the time of the plague's effective infection? What if the androids had exhibited the only signs of disturbance there would be in this area?

Then they were trapped. Those men wouldn't fall ill and leave them alone. Trapped. He thought it ironically funny that up until now he had never had any desire to return to something that once promised nothing more than the same drab passing of hours; but once his way out was taken from him, it was all he could think of.

70

I wish I were smarter, he thought. Maybe I wouldn't be so confused.

"Trouble?"

It was Lupozny, standing on the far side of the back door, his eyes narrowed in an attempt to follow Parric's line of sight.

"No, no trouble. Just thinking is all."

"Relax, brother Parric," Ike said. "There's not much any of us can do about it. We're all of us stuck. Us with our funny dummies and them with their fear and pride."

Parric looked at the smaller man, but Ike found nothing fascinating in staring at trees and left the room.

Fear. Sure, he thought, that's it right in the head. The question is, who's afraid the most? Or did it really matter?

He watched the morning glare into noon, shrink the shadows toward him. He tried keeping his mind a blank to goad the time into moving faster toward night, but images of maps with spreading red, mourning black, intruded and made him think in spite of himself of the disasters his people had inflicted upon themselves in the name of faith, salvation, and the glory of the greater good.

If there was anything that should have truly united the race, it was the *Alpha*, but starships take too long going and coming. Though the crew was multinational, all countries claimed it for their own, the idea of sharing nebulous glory apparently as alien as the stars *Alpha* would hopefully visit.

There had been a few moments in the past thirty-six hours when Jessica had almost made him feel wrong in his condemnation of the race's failures, but those times were scattered and bitterly interrupted by her continuing puzzling attitude toward him. She had almost solved his riddle when the Oraton men arrived, and he considered confronting her again before deciding against it. If it were important, he thought, she would tell him sooner or later.

Moving away from his post, he rubbed his eyes and stretched, not realizing how stiff he had become, how still he had remained throughout the afternoon. He was surprised, then, to see it was dusk.

"Yes, sir," he said as he rounded the table, "the faithful watchdog. Arf."

Chapter 6

Jessica was crouched on the lounge. The drapes were tied to one side and she was staring intently out into the street. Ike sat beside her, using the second window to watch the opposite end of Town. Parric stood in the entryway, frowning, thinking that perhaps they had fallen into the same dreamlike state as he, but their attitudes were wrong. Jessica was holding tightly to the edge of the lounge with one hand, the other working monotonously at the shank of hair she had fastened behind her head. It was an awkward position, but she seemed oblivious to discomfort. Ike, on the other hand, could not keep still. He bounced one foot on the floor, shifted his buttocks continuously as he ducked his head and stretched his neck as though trying to get a closer look at what he was watching.

A quick, second-thought look at the wall showed Parric the comunit was still on but the volume gone, the picture yet gray.

"Jess," he started, but she hushed him and beckoned quickly.

Instinctively bending low, he almost crawled on his

knees until he was able to squeeze next to her between the window and the lounge. She pointed, but he could not take his eyes from her face: white, her cheeks indenting as she sucked at air, her jaw thrust out, then in toward her chest.

"It's happened," she whispered, and Parric immediately thought the Oraton men were succumbing to the plague. When he looked outside, he wondered how much more wrong he could get.

Across the street in the yard directly opposite were Dorski and Fabor, struggling. They were standing, their arms clasped tightly around each other's waist. Their faces were dead in the dimming light, as expressionless as the androids now lying impotent behind the clinic; yet he could sense the straining of manufactured muscles, the tearing that must be going on at joints and meticulously soldered junctures of intricate wiring.

"How long?" he asked, not realizing he was whispering, too.

"At least half an hour," Ike said, his orator's voice hoarse as if he had been screaming. "That's when Jess first saw them. They came out of the house—"

"And just stood there," Jessica finished. "All of a sudden they just grabbed and that's all they've done since."

"They'll destroy each other," Parric said, standing.

"What do you think you're going to do, walk right up and separate them? Maybe talk to them like you always do?" Ike turned his head to let Parric see the full range of his contempt. "Sit down, brother doc. There's nothing you can do but watch. You want to bet a little on the outcome? A week's credits on the skinny one."

Parric hesitated but Jessica lent him no guidance and it wasn't long before he crouched again.

The androids had dropped to their knees, their balance threatened as they swayed from side to side, barely righting themselves to sway again. Searching further along the street, Parric saw the Warners standing with Mrs. Keller on her porch. They were in shadow, but their heads were turned toward the struggle.

Gone, he thought. I should have tried harder to get them to the clinic instead of letting them go.

Suddenly there was a report Parric first thought was a rifle firing at the fighters, but when his scanning of the hillside was fruitless and he returned his gaze to the lawn, he saw Fabor bending Dorski backward. Jessica shuddered, turned away when Dorski's clothes pulled out of his trousers and Parric could see the ripping split along his stomach.

"Broke his goddamn back," Ike said. "Damn! I should have made that bet."

Fabor let the still-moving Dorski drop to the ground, then paused only a moment before plunging his hands into the fallen android's abdominal cavity, yanking fiercely until gleaming threads of three centuries of science spilled to the grass.

Parric heard a choking behind him, grimaced at a whiff of acrid nausea. He was sympathetic to Jessica's reaction but could not let himself dismiss what had happened quite yet. He leaned as close as he could to the window, trying to see through the hazy darkness exactly what Fabor was doing. The android was still on its knees, pulling, examining, tossing away. Ike was swearing.

And suddenly Parric got to his feet.

"Now what?" the cameraman said.

"The clinic," Parric said, heading for the kitchen.

"Fabor's indulging in a little self-realization. He's learning in a few minutes what most of us couldn't understand in a lifetime."

"What the hell are you talking about?"

Ike followed him; Jessica, though still trembling from her shock, hurried after.

"If he learns too much about what makes himself tick, Ike," Parric said, turning out all the house's light from a main switch in the kitchen, "then he might try to activate the rest of the Town."

"I thought they knew all there was to know about themselves."

Parric shook his head. "How much do you know about the way you function? Not a hell of a lot, I imagine, but more than the average man; and that's what those things are supposed to be, remember?"

"My god, what a fine bunch of idiots they were that turned those things loose."

"Maybe," Parric said, knowing he was stalling but unable to take the final step, "but we can't argue about that now. You stay here with Jessica and for God's sake don't let any of them in. So far, Fabor's the only one that's gone bad. The others, though, aren't or can't be far behind. I've got to stop them from getting a tidy little army together."

"What are you going to do?" Jessica said.

"Destroy the diagunit."

"Hold it, brother," Ike said, spitting a gum wad into his palm and tossing it into a corner. "If you do that, you won't be able to put the rest out of commission."

"Tell you what," Parric said, "you go out there and order them down to the clinic, okay? You tell them old Doc Parric wants to see them and see how far it gets you."

76

They were silent, then, and Parric used it to break away from Ike's grip on his arm and open the door. "Wait for me," he said, "but not for long. If they come at you, go for their eyes first, then their hips."

Not waiting to see if they understood, he closed the door and dropped to the grass, pressing tightly against the house as he crawled to the end of the house. It would be a few minutes more before the streetlamps snapped on, and in the fuzzy distortion of not-quite-evening, he hoped the hunters still prowling the hills would not be able to notice him. Plucking at his shirt absently, he silently thanked Fate for allowing him to keep his black clothes on. For once, they didn't make him seem overly morbid.

He listened, then eased over to look out across the street. It was difficult to see anything clearly, but there were figures moving and the crackling of metal rubbing fragilely against itself. Still learning, he thought and pushed himself to his feet. He waited a second longer, then dashed across the lawn, hurdling a small bush, not stopping to see if he had been spotted. Ducking low, sprinting after a spill over an unseen obstacle, it was three blocks before his chest began to ache, his side beginning a throbbing he knew would soon twist into rippling pain. At the fourth block he pulled up to a walk, paying no attention to the houses since these no longer served as dwellings, watching instead for long minutes the street that had finally broken into islands of light. There were still no sounds of pursuit though he was positive his clumsy running had more than served as a beacon for those who had once been his friends. With one hand pressed tightly against his waist, he rested against the last house and stared across the side-street to the clinic yard. There was no movement that he could see, nothing besides the coursing of his blood that his ears could hear. Faintly the images of the deadened androids strewn in the yard became recognizable and, after telling himself that if he didn't move now it was all over but the screaming, he ran for the back door.

Down the curb, over the thin layer of tarmac, up again, and he stumbled over a leg, sprawled with hands groping toward nothing. His shoulder struck a head. There was a century of panic as he struggled to release himself from the corpselike grip of one of Coates' children, standing, stepping away, and falling again, this time to reach out and grip the unyielding breast of someone's android wife. His palms, lips, forehead slick with perspiration as he rolled over onto his hands and knees and crawled to the door, unlocked it, and fell inside into a deeper blackness. He sobbed once, pulled his legs under him, and used the inner wall to prop him to his feet. Instinctively, he extended a hand to switch on the light, then checked himself and felt his way to the front.

There was nothing that he could see that might have been threatening. The Keller house was too far away and back in shadow, and he couldn't tell if the porch was still occupied. The immediate area was deserted, however, and he gave himself a moment's rest before working his way back into the office. Time, he realized, was not about to freeze the universe and pave his way to safety unaided. With motions he had thought many times he could do with his eyes closed, he dragged the diagunit from the closet and began feeling for the hatches that led to its heart. A simple matter of extracting a few wires, he thought, and tearing loose some circuitry. Simple. Too simple.

He heard the humming, realized he had been listening to it for too long without understanding what it was.

In the front, and its monotonic relentlessness prevented him from guessing how many were coming.

Stepping back, he considered trying to escape at once, and the grinning lips of Lupozny burst from some barrel in his mind. Banging once against the side of his desk, he reached around and picked up the chair he had used when he spoke with Jessica the day she had arrived. He hefted it over his shoulder, waited until its weight began to pull it down, then forced the momentum with a push/pull of his arms.

Shattering.

He was thrown back against the wall as the diagunit's power source protested the invasion, sparked, and popped in a dizzying array of minor explosions. Not waiting to see if he had been completely successful, Parric ran out the back, his way over the bodies of the androids sporadically lightened by the unit's convulsive dying. Caution then dropped behind him when he heard a shout, another and another. Veering around the corner, he raced along the street, believing the hard surface would do him better than the give of the ground. Something hissed past him, struck a tree trunk, and clattered into his path, causing him to leap higher than necessary. He stopped, turned, and picked up a metal leg torn from a chair. He brandished it and turned to run again, stopped when he saw the Keller boy standing in front of him.

"Hi, son," he said. "It's only Doc Parric."

The android didn't answer, and Parric could hear the others running closer behind him.

"Only Doc Parric," he said again, took two steps forward, and lunged, plunging the leg into the boy's right eye. The android reached up, too late, to grab the weapon and Parric swung it against the other lens before jumping out of the range of its grasping.

As he had run from the men of Oraton, he now used the trees to protect himself from the fiercely thrown objects the androids had picked up. But he was twice struck in the back, a third time threw him to the ground. He called out, rolled onto his back and, without thinking, kicked out at the diving figure of Fabor. The android was thrown to one side but was on its feet before Parric could shake off the stinging that temporarily immobilized him. Dragging himself, tense against anticipated blows, he called out again, heard a door slam, and saw Ike race from the porch.

"Come on," the cameraman said, blowing out breath as he tried to help Parric to his feet. "Come on, damn it, come on!"

After slipping once and nearly going down, Parric finally managed an arm around Lupozny's waist and they stumbled in a three-legged race to the front door.

"Fabor," Parric said when they reached the steps. "Be careful . . ."

Ike pushed him ahead and turned around. "Nothing. They've stopped."

Parric wanted to argue, but Jessica had already come outside and was pulling him hysterically. A final shove from Ike and they were inside, dropping to the floor.

"Damn," Ike said, shaking his head as he pulled himself to sit against the wall. "I don't believe what I just saw. I don't believe it." He looked as though he were about to cry, but Jessica had already begun, tears washing her face, hugging Parric until he thought he would have to strike her to make her release him.

"Relax," he finally gasped. "I'm all right."

"I know," she said, still crying.

"Brother Parric," Ike said, "we've got to get out of here."

"No. We can't leave. Not now."

He ignored Lupozny's protests as he disentangled himself from Jessica's arms and hurried into the living room where he dropped to the floor and looked out.

"But why?" Ike demanded, crouching beside him, tugging at one shoulder.

"You saw, idiot. We wouldn't get two steps from this house before they'd be on us."

"Listen—"

"Shut up and look."

Mrs. Keller was standing on the sidewalk, her hands limp at her side, her face turned toward the house, leaving no doubt that she was watching. On the left-hand corner was Mr. Warner, on the right was his wife. Watching, unmoving, remaining far enough from the light to appear as though they were garbed in black. A smaller figure, Mrs. Keller's son, wandered along the street, arms, hands, fingers wavering in front of him, a low wail trailing. Mrs. Keller didn't move, and the boy passed on.

"He'll hit the barrier," Parric said, his voice low, "and probably get turned around. Unless one of them guides him, he'll be completely helpless."

Ike only grunted. "Say," he said suddenly, pointing, "looks like you did all right for yourself."

"I didn't—" And Parric stopped, spotting the twisted Fabor sprawled where they had fought. "I couldn't have, Ike. I only kicked at him once, and I was lying down." He put one hand to the glass, wiping, hoping the movement would bring him an answer, but the android remained as he saw it, the clothes shredded at the hips, its head ripped off.

"Frank?"

He forced himself to focus on Jessica's face.

"I looked in the back, Frank, and I can't see anyone. I saw light, though, reflecting somewhere. I think maybe something's burning."

"The clinic," he said simply and hurried an explanation of what he had done.

"Got to hand it to you, clerk," Ike said. "I don't think I would have had the nerve to stick around. We heard that singing, or whatever you call it, and we spent most of the time trying to dig holes in the floor."

"Believe me, it wasn't nerve. I don't even remember what made me do it. I just did it and ran."

"Well, you took one of them with you and that evens the odds a bit."

"One," Parric said, "is one too many."

"Frank," Jessica said, "what do we do now?"

"Leave. Fast," Ike said, moving away from the window to the chair he had settled by the barcab. "I'd rather take my chances with those gun-happy creeps than those things out there now."

"No," Parric said. "We can't go. It's too dangerous outside the Town. We could get shot, the plague—"

"Damn it, I don't understand you, Parric," Ike said. "I mean, how can there be any choice in the matter? Those androids of yours have gone absolutely out of their brains, if they have any, and we don't stand a chance at all."

82

Jessica waited until Parric had pushed the lounge out of his way and had stretched his legs along the floor before sitting back on her heels, the streetlamp glow barely reflecting her face, making it seem as if it were floating; a strand of hair fell, caught the light, and glimmered until she brushed it back. The comunit had been switched off, and there was not even the whisper of static to cover the silence that crept in from the Town.

Parric closed his eyes, a hand gripping his right thigh in hopes of strangling the ache that lurked there.

"Are you hurt?" she asked.

He wanted to say yes, shook his head instead.

"He's thinking," Ike said. "Don't you know men like him have to think before they do anything?" There was the scarcely audible click of teeth against glass, then a bubbling that followed another drink ordered.

Outside, the explosion of a shattered window.

"That does it," Ike said. "Jess, go into the kitchen and turn on the main switch. I'll need light to get our gear together."

Parric watched Jessica disappear from the glow, saw his own shadow against the wall: a head framed between thick black bars. Penitentiary. Penitent. Had he imprisoned himself in a souless Town, a solitary confinement that elevated him above a world that scorned commitment? Or had he locked the world out because he had felt helpless, too helpless to believe that an individual could do more than make a feeble gesture, and afraid that gesture would be received with indifference?

Nonsense, he told himself. Safety first, damn it.

The lights flickered on, erasing the prison image,

and he blinked as Jessica returned to dial the room dark again, leaving only a slash from the back room. He turned his head and saw the three androids had not moved. Dix he could see nowhere and, after a minute's confused thought, realized he hadn't seen Keller's eldest girl child since the pressure began. Using the sill for balance, he pushed himself to his feet, swaying until his legs stiffened.

He heard Ike swearing.

He heard another window shatter.

"Frank, what are you going to do?"

She was standing beside him, close but not touching.

"I was thinking of staying, actually—"

"But you can't, not with—"

"—but I've changed my mind."

"Why?" Quietly.

He thought: because if it looks like I'm going to die, I'd just as soon die with people around me, even if it's the people who kill me.

He said: "Because you still haven't answered my question."

She smiled, touched his arm briefly, and turned as Ike came out of the bedroom festooned with his equipment.

"Help," he said.

"Forget it," said Parric, and Jessica nodded. "He's right, Ike. We can't take it all with us."

"Do you know how much this stuff costs?" Ike almost yelped at the painful thought and crammed a wad of gum into his mouth. "And most of it isn't even mine, for crying out loud."

A rock interrupted him, smashing through a front window. Parric shoved Jessica to one side before dropping to the floor. Ike was motionless, his eyes wide, his jaw still as the stone struck the wall next to him and rebounded against his foot.

"How fast can you move?" Parric said.

Ike stared at the floor as if he were looking at his reflection in the angles of broken glass. Then he kicked the rock to one side and littered the area around him with cases and cameras.

"One," he said, fixing a small tricorder to his belt. "For history."

"If there is one," Parric said, "and assuming there is, for us at least, I suggest we move to the back where we won't get brained."

A moment later, Jessica was at the back door, shaking her head to Lupozny's unasked question after she made a quick reconnaissance of the yard.

"Consider," Parric said, his fingers stroking the thumbslot of the door, "our hunter friends are still out there probably, and most likely sticking close to the north end of Town, assuming that's the way we have to get out. I remember when I first came here, I thought the casings had something to do with the way you got in and out. But with the patchkey we can leave from anywhere, and I suggest down by the clinic."

"Good," Ike said. "Then we'll head for whatsitsname, Oraton, and find the first comunit that works. We can call out from there and let someone in charge know we're all right."

"No," Jessica said. "That's the worst thing we can do. If that place is up in arms, we wouldn't last a very long time."

She looked to Parric, who nodded.

"So what do we do? Find a cozy mountaintop and turn into hermits or something?"

Another pane splintered and something heavy thudded against the front entrance.

"Out," Parric said. "Our time's up."

Without waiting for comment, he slid open the door and pushed Jessica out, followed quickly with Ike's hand in the small of his back for guidance. There was a moon, but faint, and they could see where they were going though only enough to successfully avoid those objects large and substantial in the gray light. At the edge of the house, he looked toward the main street and saw Mrs. Warner walking away from her post. He shook a cautioning hand until she had passed from sight, then grabbed Jessica's wrist and started running. He heard nothing but their feet thudding into the dirt and grass, tympani to the cracking of wood. He cursed, thinking the sudden increase in bodies would alert the hunters, but still hoped the men would be used to seeing the clinic yard cluttered with androids; they had probably not counted them and wouldn't notice three more, if they were given the time to move slowly.

Ike passed him, slowed, and matched his pace. Parric wanted to give him a reassuring smile, but his mouth was wide open, sucking in air that seemed not to be sufficient for his burning lungs. He stumbled once, shook off a hand at his elbow, and instantly regretted it when he saw Jessica grin.

A scream diffused the silence, more now like a protracted wailing. Jessica faltered and he shoved his hand against her shoulder, spilling her when they reached the back of the clinic.

The three of them fell, then, rolling onto their backs, their mouths into funnels as their chests heaved. A minute later, still unable to understand the source of the scream, Parric twisted to his stomach and began a crawl

86

to the barrier, his eyes intent on trying to keep the hill's cover from swaying. His hands reached out, grabbed like talons while his feet pushed, slipping, once kicking Ike on the shoulder. Again his hand stretched out, and was stopped. Pulling himself up to sit, he reached into his pocket.

"Oh, damn," he whispered as Ike and Jessica came up beside him. "I must have lost my key back there on the street."

"To the rescue," Jessica said and pulled out the patchkey that had given her access the day before. "No," she said when he reached for it. "I'll do it."

He wanted to argue, decided against it when he realized their forms were more than suspiciously huddled together should one of the hunters look their way. Stung that his brief period of leadership had stumbled at a crucial point, he slid to one side and let Ike pass when Jessica inserted the key into the barrier, causing the momentary disturbance that allowed them to pass it freely. Twice more, and his skin was tingling, his hair feeling as if it were standing on end. He shook himself as he scrambled across the cleared section of the perimeter, his hands automatically kept away from his sides in unreasonable fear that a touch would electrocute him.

An explosion he could feel through the ground, and he stood, not thinking, watching as his house ignited in a fire rain. The trees prevented him from seeing it all, but his imagination told him the androids were dancing around the flaming ruins, singing Dix's song.

And he offered no resistance when Ike roughly grabbed at his arms and yanked him to shelter behind a sprawling bush. In spite of his running, a cowering hope had remained that the androids would not harm the Town, had only been demented enough to want to get at him. When the house next to his flared, died in the same fashion, he turned away and cradled his head on his upraised knees.

Chapter 7

It was a satin dark under the wide-set trees and rambling brush, yet light enough for each to see dimly the other's still form, and it wasn't long before Ike and Jessica had crowded close to Parric, who would not move.

"Now what?" Ike said, almost in dusgust, as he shook Parric's shoulder, trying to get him to lift his head.

"Leave him alone. Can't you see he's hurt?" She pushed at him until he stopped, but made no comforting gestures of her own.

"Hurt? How? Where?"

"Not that way," she said angrily. "Just leave him alone for a minute. We're safe enough for the time being."

Parric remained silent, his eyes closed and adding to the black that returned as the second house's fire faded to a glow. There was an outburst of summoning yells at the far side of the Town, from the outside and growing fainter as they moved away. A shot that might have been a signal, renewed calling and two shots more. Footsteps, and several running men, heedless of their noise, approached and passed them without pausing in the wakes of erratic beams of flashlight. Parric stiffened at the sounds, listened to the mindless crashing, and imagined the crush of giants kicking at anthills. He saw the Town as it had been, probably would have been had not those ants aspired to become more than they were. He gulped for air and choked, raising his head to look between the leaves at the sky. A sustained hush of wind brushed branches aside and the moon stared back at him, a bulging half, flanked low by a solitary star. For a moment he thought it had moved, closer perhaps, becoming larger, swelling into the ungainly, complicated beauty that comprised the *Alpha's* component superstructure. He blinked, then, and the star was only a star.

Wrong again, he thought, not ants, and he was suddenly chagrined that he should have demeaned those who had built the starship, insulted those who lived within her. Not ants, but children.

"Hey, listen," Lupozny said impatiently, "do you think maybe we can get out of here now, or are we waiting for a sign?"

Jessica's hand moved faster than either man could see, and the retort of her slap turned them into statues, startled Parric, who immediately strained to search out the possible betrayal of stalking men. A minute later, he allowed himself to breath when he heard nothing but the nocturnal staccato of invisible insects and the rustling of a handful of stirring birds in the foliage above him. The shouting had completely died away, and the shots' echoes reverberated only in his mind.

He cleared his throat and the two reporters huddled closer.

"The question is not, if you'll excuse me, whether or

not we go, but where we go once we get started." He hurried then when he felt Ike shift to interrupt. "Somehow or other those men were lured away. They probably thought the explosions were diversions or cover of some kind and we've already slipped out. They were probably just shooting at shadows." He stopped, swallowed the bile that rose toward his mouth before continuing. "And I still think it's a bad idea to head for Oraton."

"Why?" Ike said. "There's people there."

"Exactly, and that's why we can't go. Look, Ike, Oraton is the nearest regular town to us, and if those men knew about what we were doing, thought they knew rather, then it stands to reason that the whole town believes the same thing. We're strangers, Ike, and can't take the chance of getting ourselves into more than we can handle."

"He means killed, whitehead," Jessica said. "Come on, you've seen what happens in a riot. Remember that food thing we went to in MexiSector a couple of years ago? What did that mob do to those men they thought were ContiGov agents?"

Parric didn't ask. Since his troubles had begun, his imagination had been working too much overtime.

Ike grunted. "All right. Then what do we do about the plague?"

"If we're infected," Parric said, "there's nothing we can do. But Floyd said the odds were good that we're all right, and I agree with him."

"Listen, I thought that doctor stuff was all for show. How can you tell?"

Parric reached out and slapped his left bicep. Ike hissed and shoved the hand away. "I can't for sure," he said, "but first, you've been favoring that arm since you got here. I know your camerapak was heavy, but not so much that you had to carry it the way you did. You got shots before you came, right? And I'll bet a year's credits there was an antidote in them, and I'll double that if you two aren't damned special for some reason that you got it."

"But that was days ago," Ike protested, "Coates didn't tell us about the plague until yesterday."

"That doesn't mean he didn't know about it," Jessica said. "It stands to reason they'd want to protect the government as soon as they got wind of the details of the plague and the war news, which obviously the top had before it broke it to the public. They were hedging, just in case. Remember, he said antidotes were popping up all over."

"And," said Parric, "you two got it because you'd already been chosen to come into a Town where androids would be particularly sensitive to the virus, or whatever a plague is."

"Okay," Ike said. "I'll assume for the sake of my bad heart that you two are right. Then what about you, brother Parric?"

He would not answer immediately. He had been talking without thinking, mainly in an effort to calm himself as much as to quiet the others. The mention of the possibility of his own infection, however, did not have the anticipated reaction; he was not afraid, not as much as resigned to yet another struggle.

"I'm not sure," he said when Jessica prodded him, "but I suspect it's pretty much run its course. You see, Floyd was wrong when he said the plague had passed over day before yesterday because I had already noticed several bits of behavior that were unusual as early as yesterday morning before I went to the clinic. I didn't make the connection until just now. If effects show up in something less, but not much less, than forty-eight hours and are almost always fatal, then by rights, if I have it, I should be dead.''

He grinned, not that they would see him in the near-total darkness, but because he suddenly felt a dozen years younger. He wasn't at all positive that his conclusions were correct, but at the moment they were all he had.

"I hate to keep playing the rat," Ike said finally, "but how do you know you won't contract it out here? Maybe there's some of it still lying around."

"The birds," Parric said. "They're warmblooded and still very alive."

"That doesn't mean—"

"All right," Jessica said sharply. "Enough, please! We could go on like this all night and we won't have to worry about the damned plague—we'll either get shot or starve to death."

In spite of himself, Parric laughed and found it was difficult to stop.

"Hey, take it easy," Ike said. "We still have to get out, you know. I believe you were about to tell us humble reporters how."

"A Town," Parric said. "Like mine, that is. Jess is right about Oraton, and I'd guess that holds for nearly every other human community around here. None of them are very large, mostly holdouts against the cities. If they haven't been wiped out, they're immunized and more than likely fortified. And we, as strangers, are prime targets for the hatred you saw this afternoon. I suggest heading for Cam McLeod. He's more levelheaded than me and will be bound to know what to do next, especially until we contact Floyd again."

"And what if we can't?"

"Later," Jessica said. "First things first. We've wasted too much time already, and those men will be back when they see it wasn't us they were shooting at."

There was a hesitation born of reluctance to leave what had proven to be, however temporary, a haven, and to abandon what had once been a landmark of a world unchanged by disaster. Parric was tempted to slip back inside, hide from men and androids until he was either killed or rescued, but the moment proved resistible and he slipped between them to begin the climb.

The underbrush was less of an obstacle than he had feared. Though heavy, it was for the most part clumped, and he was able to walk rapidly without too many sidetracks. The cloudless night made it easier, outlining his brief glimpses of the summit to give him direction, occasionally finding a break in the cover large enough to aid him in avoiding thrashing through thickets that would give them away as surely as if they had carried torches. Absently, as he walked, he checked his watch, noting it was still lacking midnight, and not until later did he understand how much had happened in so short a time.

The hill steepened and he began using branches and brush to pull himself upward. He cursed at the aching in his thighs and ankles, once reaching down to wrench up a rock that had tripped him and fling it as far as he could into the blackness. He found a path, too narrow to be manmade, and followed it down the opposite side, across a hollow similar to the one they had just left and up again. His hands were burning, his arms stinging from the beelike stings of whipped branches. His clothes dampened and became a second skin that chaffed and increased the sense of pain whenever he was careless.

And finally, after cresting a third and lower hill, he slumped to the ground, his back against a tree, and waited for the others.

Ike stretched out beside him, his arms hugging his chest as he gasped for larger portions of air.

Jessica folded to her knees, bent forward and retched dryly, one hand grabbing at her hair to keep it from her face.

"They didn't look so high when the sun was up," Ike said, rasping. "This is ridiculous, brother Parric. We'll never make it."

"You're soft," Jessica said without accusing. "But there must be a better way than this."

"It was dumb to even start," Parric agreed, "especially at night. We're just not the wilderness types."

"Daylight, then," Ike said, and when no one objected, he rolled onto his side and immediately fell asleep.

Jessica crawled to sit next to Parric, shivering as the night's chill breezed across her sweat-soaked skin. She pressed against his side and, when he shifted his arm, pulled it across her shoulders.

"Don't get excited," she said. "I'm cold."

Parric ignored her, content for the moment to feel his lungs return to their normal size, the knifelike ripping in his chest reduced to a dulling ache.

"You know, every morning," he said, not looking to see if she were listening, "I used to walk to the clinic and watch them. Sometimes I'd invite myself to breakfast and make notes if something didn't seem right. After a while, it got so I didn't have to be on my guard

95

all the time. Everything seemed so natural, it wasn't long before I hated taking their backs off, poking around with things I barely understood. It destroyed the illusion, I guess, and I suppose it was a good thing. But I hated it just the same."

"I wonder," she said sleepily, "what's going on in the real world?"

"Who knows," Parric said. "If ContiGov was moving, I'd imagine there's a hell of a lot of deterioration in the cities. Looters, ghouls, local anarchy. The small-towns that have survived have probably set themselves up as self-sufficiently as they can. I wouldn't be surprised if some of them will even issue script."

"But communications haven't broken down . . ."

"Assuming our case was isolated, maybe not, but when all you get is a voice telling you everything is all right while, at the same time, you see your neighbors dropping on the street, the reaction should be obvious. And if you've been inoculated but the face on the screen won't tell you a thing other than what you've been hearing for days, you either shut it off or put a boot through it. Either way, it looks like the new password is distrust, especially . . ."

"What?" she said when he stopped and cocked his head.

"Nothing. I thought I heard something. Told you I wasn't the wilderness type. What I was going to say was, especially when there's a good chance some android's gotten out and is making things even more unsettled."

"You don't know any got out," she said, stirring against his chest.

"True, but it's bound to happen. One, two, some of the others will shut down just as Floyd told them, only they'll go too far and cut the barriers, too. We panicked and got out before we could do anything. Who knows about the rest?''

"Who knows?" she repeated and her head slid down into his lap.

Parric arched his back away from the tree, then squirmed until the jab of bark was bearable. He didn't want to close his eyes and admit the sleep that stung. He tried instead to find a reason for running, one that would make sense in the preservation of his life; and it was *Alpha*, as it had always been. Should the world not recover, should someone get mad and unleash yet another attack somewhere with fuses that would ignite everywhere, something had to be left for them to find, even if it was only a suddenly confused insurance clerk and two reporters.

You're too pessimistic, he thought. The world will survive as it always has.

But as what? he wanted to know. The *Alpha* needs more than an underground government and tiny pockets of armed and frightened men. It deserves more, has to have more, and at Cam's we'll keep things sane and prepare for the worst.

He agreed, pleased, then felt a heavy body shifting across his legs, pinning him to the ground. He twisted, trying to shove it away, his arms flailing until his head snapped back against the tree and he opened his eyes. Jessica was pushing herself up, staring at him as she backed away.

"I . . ." He shook his head and gently massaged pain the tree had given him. "I thought . . . I think . . . I must have been dreaming."

"Nice," she said, circling in front of him to wake Ike.

"I hope it wasn't about me."

"No, it was about—"

"Hey," Ike said, sitting up, brushing at his hair to free the clinging bits of dirt and leaves. "Don't tell me it's morning already."

Parric looked up to the sky, starless as the first light sponged away the black. The air remained chilled, but the warmth of the coming day could be felt already driving the dampness back, and a pair of drab-feathered birds squawked away from them.

"I'm hungry," Ike said.

"Later," said Parric. "We've got to get to McLeod as soon as possible. On the way we might find something to eat."

"That sounds really great, brother. And how do we get to this magical friend of yours?"

"Walk."

"Maybe not," Jessica said. "Frank, do you think those hunters walked all the way from Oraton?"

Parric considered the terrain he'd seen when they had flown him in, then shook his head. "I doubt it. They must have had some kind of vehicle. The Town is too tucked away."

Ike looked back the way they had come during the night. "For once, Parric, I agree with you. And even if they are in better shape than us, they were probably too anxious to get their dirty work done."

"Right. Look," Parric said, pointing toward the west, "that's the way we have to go. I remember a map on Floyd's office, the Towns on it being in the shape of sort of a question mark. I was near the bottom, Cam about halfway up. I know from coming in that there's a road nearby. We ought to hike down there and see what we can come up with."

"You think they just left it there for us to find?"

"I don't think anything," Parric said, angry at the sneer not restricted to Lupozny's voice. "But they may not have left the area of the Town yet, waiting for full dawn so they can check. Now there might also be some already following, and I think we'd be better off moving."

He watched as Ike scratched through his white hair, then turned to head down the slope. Jessica followed immediately, both paying little attention to Lupozny's protests, most of which centered around waiting until he had worked out the stiffness he had inherited from sleeping on the ground.

"Is he always like that?" Parric said.

"Funny, he wonders the same about you."

Then why, he asked himself, do they bother to stay with him? It certainly wasn't because of his leadership abilities, nor was it for the strength to see them through a crisis that persisted in behaving like a dream; it could have been that they were frightened by his cynical estimates of the disaster's extent and had succumbed to the instinct of safety in numbers. Whatever, he thought, but it would be a lot easier if Lupozny would only stop carping.

Progress in the sunlight was almost too rapid for adjustment. The hill's outergrowth had lost its lurking sinister cast, and had become instead a fascinating collection of tall and stunted trees that had long since adapted to the once poisonous air and were now in the process of reversing themselves. Parric grinned to himself, thinking of their confusion, then stumbled down a grassy bank to the shoulder of the road almost before he knew it was there.

Quickly, he scrambled back into the woods and

leaned against a trunk. When Ike caught up, he shook his head in evident surprise that Parric actually found what they were looking for. Remembering the cameraman's previous reluctant compliments, Parric wished he would make up his mind so they would know where they stood and could behave accordingly.

"Right or left?" Jessica asked when she saw no one was going to make a decision.

"Right, I should think," Parric said before Ike could answer. "They wouldn't want to get too close in case we had some kind of supersecret, deadly warning system ready to fry them if they stepped on the wrong rock."

"They were that scared of you?" Ike said.

"You saw them," Jessica said. "What do you think?"

Ike shrugged. "Do we split up?"

"Don't know," Parric said. "It would probably be wiser to, but if one of us gets caught, considering our stealthy travels thus far, the others won't be far behind. We might as well all go."

"You're the boss," Jessica said.

"Why not?" Ike said, stepping out from the trees.

The road was not a major route, being comprised mostly of crushed rock heavily embedded in hardened dirt. Its brushed look suggested it was mainly used by hovercats, but it wasn't so rough that landcars could be entirely ruled out.

With Jessica in the middle and Ike behind, they strung out along the irregular slash in the hills and walked as fast as their rapidly numbing legs would allow. Frequent curves, rises, and dips prevented them from seeing too far ahead, but Parric thought they should easily be able to hear anyone approaching now that they were not thrashing through the forest like blind men. He looked down at his feet, watching them appear and vanish as he walked, almost immediately yielding to an illusion of floating when he could no longer feel the road beneath him. He was grateful that the sun was still climbing over the mountains beyond the hills, keeping the area in shadow and holding the temperature down to a level he could tolerate. He had been spoiled, he knew, by the Town's recycled and cooled system, and a low wash of envy for Jessica and Ike momentarily covered him. They, at least, would not feel the heat as sensitively as he.

"Here," Jessica said suddenly, pointing to something on the side under an overhanging bank.

Parric turned, squinting, and saw a small brown creature lying in a viciously contorted position beneath a bush. He didn't know what the animal was, but he knew what it had died of from the obscenely ugly welts that had been torn open wherever the creature's claws could reach. Its head was buried in deeper shadow, but he knew without looking that it had most likely torn out its own throat scratching at the plague.

"It's come and gone," Jessica said, mainly for his benefit. Then she hugged herself and hurried away while Ike bent for a closer examination.

"Beautiful," he said, straightening after a second to rejoin Parric. "Now I can imagine what people look like." Again his face paled and, as dark eyes stared into light, his head ducked in as close to an apology as his temperament would allow. "Let's go, doc," he said.

"For once, I don't think I want to—"

A shout, and they broke into a sprint, suddenly aware that Jessica had left them alone. Another call, and the recognition of their names lashed them into a headlong run that nearly brought them unchecked against the battered hulk of a landcar. Jessica was walking slowly around it, leaning over to look inside. It was an ancient, narrow, two-seater, scooped low in front and back, its gray windows streaked with grime. Only its large thick tires so obviously new hinted it had not been merely abandoned.

"Lovely," Ike said, trying to lift the side doors, cursing when he found them locked. "Still lovely, though."

"You shouldn't have yelled like that," Parric said. "They might have heard you."

She waved away the scolding and shaded her eyes with her hands as she searched the road to its bend. "It was hidden in that clump of bushes over there," she said, pointing. "You can see where the branches are flattened, and the grass. Someone pushed it out here."

"Nice," Ike said.

"Well, you'd better get in somehow," she said. "This place isn't going to stay lonely forever."

"No easier said than done," Ike boasted. He snapped a narrow branch from a sapling and stripped it before poking it through a strip of insulation between glass and door frame. "They've been making these things for hundreds of years and still haven't figured out a way to keep thieves like me from opening them." With an unnecessary flourish, he tossed away the branch and lifted the door, swinging it up and locking it like a bird's broken wing.

"Genius," Parric said, slipping into the driver's seat. "The trouble is, I can't drive one of these things, and even if I could, there isn't a key."

"You drive hover, right?" Ike said as Parric climbed out again and nodded. "Then no problem. Practically the same, only you don't have to worry so much about drift as you do staying on the damned road. Now this little deathtrap," he continued as he lay on the front floor and lifted a panel under the dash, "has, if I remember correctly, three alternate wiring systems. One is for the regular ignition, one for emergencies that starts with a tiny key propped inside here—damn, it's gone! Oh, well, there's a third the manufacturer sticks in in case the owner wants—damn, this is tight!—to add a few dozen extras. Did you know for a while there you could actually mount machine guns in here, back during the Ghetto War?"

Parric could only make noises of interest. He was getting nervous, standing out in broad daylight waiting for someone unseen to shoot him down without first discovering how harmless he was. He asked Ike to hurry, was brusquely assured that everything would be fine if he were only left in peace to make a few illegal cross connections. Parric backed away, then, to look at the landcar, seeing beneath the country patina of rusted age and thousands of kilometers of abusive driving a once-green shine that would have reflected the trees it passed under in a deep-forest hue. He told himself, under Ike's muffled swearing, that he should feel guilty about taking it, was not entirely unpleasantly surprised that he wasn't, and decided it was because its owner was out to cut short his suddenly interesting life. He thought of McLeod and the hoarse rough laughter that had brightened the training sessions and exasperated the instructors. He had laughed at Parric's hopes for the *Alpha*, but only skeptically, not derisively. He had not withdrawn into the Town as Parric had done, and his constant badgering of the Central, Parric reasoned, probably made him the best informed about what had really happened and how to proceed.

Cam, he thought, you damn well better hold on until I get there.

"Frank!" Jessica had run back to the landcar, was tugging at his arm. "There's someone coming!"

"Ike," he said, bending, "hurry it up. Jess hears someone."

There was a muttering he couldn't understand, but the sense was clear: Ike was close, but not close enough.

"Keep at it, then, damn it," he said, pulling the door down until it rested unlatched against the frame. Then he pulled Jessica with him to crouch in front of the vehicle, his head raised to peer through the windshield to the road beyond. He listened, and heard the footsteps stumbling over the worn rock, running.

"I don't think—" he started to say, then stood in amazement as a woman in a shredded white uniform dashed around the curve, saw him, and tried to twist away. But her momentum caused her to spin and she fell instead, was not able to regain her feet before Jessica and Parric could reach her.

"Wait a minute, wait a minute!" Parric said, grabbing her bare thin arms, trying to be gentle yet not wanting her to get away from him. "Hold on, we're not going to hurt you."

The woman cringed, her dirt-smudged face wincing as if expecting a blow. Then she saw Jessica and allowed herself to lessen the struggle, though Parric could feel her muscles still taut and ready to fight. Cautiously they lifted her to her feet, held her between them as they walked back to the car. Parric quickly sketched who they were, why they were trying to start the car, but he knew much of it was missing, still less reaching the still fearful woman in her panic to escape.

At that moment the car shuddered and the engine sparked into a muffled whine. As they approached, Ike grunted and sat up, lifting the side door and climbing out shaking his left hand.

"Damn near electrocuted myself, doc. I think it'll—"

"Close your mouth," Jessica said, pushing him aside and guiding the woman into the cramped storage area in the back.

"Who—"

"Later," Parric said, sliding over to the passenger side. Ike hesitated, then jumped in, closed the door, and released the brake.

"Who is she?" he asked again.

"I don't know," Parric said, "and right now, I don't care."

Chapter 8

Though Lupozny insisted they were traveling as fast as the road and the condition of the landcar permitted, Parric continually twisted around to look behind them, trying to see through the raised boiling dust, convinced the men from Oraton would soon come striding up and casually cut them all down without a qualm. It seemed impossible to him that luck was two-sided.

Jessica, meanwhile, had calmed the woman enough to reassure her they were not going to do her harm, but it was a full hour before she sat up as best she could in the inhospitable back space and look at them without being afraid.

Her name, she said as she pulled nervously at her man-short brown hair, was Peg. She had been sent into Oraton with a team of doctors from the Kentennsee Sector Hospital to immunize that community and its neighbors against the plague. Though she begged no substantial proof, she had heard that synthidotes were being easily manufactured and had already been made available in unbelievably huge quantities. In answer to a question from Ike, she guessed inoculations had begun quietly in the cities before the so-called spillover had occurred.

"What do you mean, so-called?" said Jessica.

"A lot of military went through our labs about three weeks ago," she said. "Some of the doctors thought, after the news broke, that capsules or something like that had been smuggled into the country."

"Figures," Ike said. "Keep the public informed. How the hell did you miss that one, Jess?"

Jessica scowled, puzzling Parric with its intensity, and turned back to Peg. "What . . . I mean, how did you get out here? I mean, why?"

Peg paused to wipe at her face, and Parric saw that beneath the grime and matted hair was more a girl than a woman.

"Hey, take it easy," he said. "You don't have to say anything now. Or ever, for that matter."

She smiled, weakly, and shook her head. The team, she said, avoiding their eyes, had completed its work and was about ready to move on when the trivid's coverage broke. Reaction in Oraton was swifter and more typical than anyone had imagined, and its terrified anger found easy outlet in the white-tunicked men who had said nothing beyond the lie that a new, all-purpose vaccine had been approved for field testing. Three of the doctors had been killed instantly when their rooms were fire-bombed. Another had escaped through a window but had been burned down, lasered, before he had been gone five minutes. This she was told when a pair of men dragged her into a courthouse cell for safekeeping; they had planned on holding her until the fifth had been tracked down and returned for punishment.

"I kept trying to tell them it wasn't our fault, that we

had helped them with the shots, but one kept saying they were going to have fun." She squirmed to back away and, when she found it was impossible, grabbed at her legs and held them tightly. "I was finally brought out last night because someone had started a rumor that the plague had come anyway, and they wanted me . . . to be the first to die." Her lips pulled back from her teeth and she shuddered, then started when Ike was unable to avoid a gaping pothole. "The animals had already started dying. It was horrible to see it! And they shoved me into a room where this woman seemed to be in a coma or something. It wasn't the plague because I've seen it, but I wasn't about to tell them that. I still don't know what she had, but it wasn't the plague. I know what *that* is." She looked wild for a moment, staring at Jessica, and Parric instantly braced himself to grab for her should she try to get out of the car. "It wasn't, you know, but they didn't know it. I thought for a while, then began screaming and moaning and beating on the door like I was some kind of mad person. Then I broke a window and got out. They were afraid. They didn't chase me at first. They thought I had it. They thought I would give it to them. Most of them ran away. Before they could get up enough courage to shoot me, I had already gotten into the woods. I didn't know where I was going, but I couldn't stop running. I saw the road. Then I saw you. I don't have it, you know," she said quietly, mostly to Jessica. "I don't, really. That woman was only regular sick. She didn't have it, really she didn't. And I don't have it either. Honest. I don't. Really I don't."

Parric felt irritatingly helpless as the girl subsided into an incoherent muttering that was muffled when

Jessica shifted around to pull her close, stroking her hair and cooing meaninglessly to blunt the point of her hysteria. He lifted a hand, pulled it back to silently, lightly pound a fist against the inverted dash. He saw Ike's lips moving and wasn't sure whether he was swearing or talking to the car, which seemed finally to act its age. Its low-speed whine coughed intermittently, causing the vehicle to stumble as if the gears weren't functioning properly.

Unreal, he thought, watching the hills pass in cool shades of green, the road sweep by in monotonous brown. Except for the disrepair of the landcar, he could have been riding in any one of a dozen past decades, escaping from the relentless crush of the cities by refamiliarizing himself with what land looked like, and space and the peace that fertilized it. They could have been searching for patches of truly blue sky, delighting as Lupozny aimed his camera at half-imagined glimpses of retreating wildlife.

It could have been, but he only needed to listen to the sobs of the girl in the back to remind him. Or, to look at his hands.

They were soft, once pale in exposure only to artificial light. Now they were darker and mottled with tracks of scratches and dried rivulets of blood. His palms stung when his fingers curled, and several nails had torn to the quick. And if Ike's face was any mirror indication, his own was blotted with patches of dirt turned mud from his exertion's perspiration. He pulled at his shirt to keep it away from his skin, wishing now he had kept the loose-fitting one he usually wore. And in pulling, he noticed the splits along his forearms and across his stomach, as if he had been ambushed by a frenzy of sharp-toothed rodents.

"No wonder she was afraid when she saw us," he muttered.

"Huh?" Ike glanced over, frowning, his hands trembling in the landcar's driving cuffs as he fought to keep the vehicle on the road.

"Nothing. Thinking aloud, that's all." He nodded toward the twin steering mechanisms. "I thought you said this would be easy to drive?"

"It would be if it was in decent shape," Ike said, licking his lips when they harrowingly avoided a jutting boulder. "But it's better than walking. We couldn't have gotten this far in a day, much less a couple of hours."

Parric returned to the unassuming landscape, picturing the three, no, four of them trying to hike through the hills.

"I'm hungry," Ike said. "What are we going to do for food?"

Parric looked back to Jessica and Peg, who had finally separated and were staring out the side windows.

"The next town, not Oraton, do you know how close it is?"

Peg didn't answer. Her forehead rested against the gray glass, and though her eyes were open, he doubted she was seeing anything.

"Peg," he said, more insistently, "Peg, do you know where the next place is on this road?"

Jessica tried to warn him with a frown, but he ignored her. It was fine that they had rescued Peg from certain death, but she couldn't be allowed to become deadweight in their flight. There were too many

110

hazards, and everyone would be needed to cope with them.

"Peg," he said sharply, reaching over and poking her before Jessica could stop him. "Peg, come on, we need your help. Where is the next town? We need to get food."

She stirred, pushed herself away from the window, blinking as if she'd recently awakened from a dream-filled sleep. "I don't know," she answered, scratching a cheek, the other hand unconsciously working to pull the tangles from her hair. "We flew in and out. In Oraton they burned the copter. I think . . ." And she looked outside again, straining, squinting until she shook her head. "I'm not sure. I remember a townlet nearby with a road over a bridge. It might be the one we're on, I don't know. We didn't stop. We were too late, couldn't see anyone. Funny, because the houses looked new."

Parric sympathized with the pain that shadowed her face, but he was impatient now to keep her talking. "Look, you probably went from place to place in some kind of arranged sequence. Oraton is back there to the left. You were heading in my direction, so look at the sun and see if you can remember if you were coming from the west or not."

"Oh, yes," she said, the dead look fading from her eyes. "That much I know because our shadow was always ahead of us. We traveled only during mornings, you see, because it usually took us all day and night to do . . . to do what we had to. If this is the road we flew over, we should hit two or three places before sunset."

Parric nodded, heard Lupozny release a long-held breath and knew a moment's telepathy: the townlet Peg

111

had referred to was most likely another experimental Town, one that hugged the road to test directly the androids' chances of human acceptance. Jessica tried to extract more information, most of which was useless since the mediteam had only hovered a few minutes before resuming their travel. Peg remarked that they had been puzzled because the settlement wasn't on their itinerary.

"How far?" Parric wanted to know.

Peg shrugged. "Now that you've got me thinking, we should have been there already."

"The girl's magic," Ike said, and Parric turned to see the road take a slight dip before forking. To the left it continued into the hills, reappearing at intervals as though it had been woven into the landscape; to the right it crossed a tiny wooden footbridge and stopped. In the tongue that extended less than a hundred meters beyond the bridge were three barely distinguishable parallel grooves.

"Yes, that's it," Peg said excitedly. "I'd know it even from here."

Ike pulled the landcar to the side of the road, depressing the brake but keeping the motor running. "I don't dare stop it," he said when Parric asked if he wanted to get out and look. "If I do, I may not be able to start it again. And you'd better hurry because we're running low on fuel."

Parric nodded and, without waiting for either of the women to volunteer company, he unlocked and lifted the side door, cocked it, and climbed out.

There was nothing to see, less to hear. The stream under the bridge had long ago faded, its bed blanketed with weeds and fallen needles and leaves. As he approached the grooves, he felt none of the anticipatory residual electricity and knew at once the barrier was down, either by design or accident. Using the grass-cushioned shoulder to quiet his footsteps, he passed into the Town proper, moving hurriedly as he searched the two short blocks for signs of their inhabitants. There were three houses, an all-purpose government store, and what he supposed was the clinic. He tried every door, and all were unlocked, all buildings empty, all except the last.

When he finally decided to check the clinic's examining room, he shoved aside the door, immediately wheeled around and gagged. The floor was littered with the bodies of half a dozen mangled androids, each torn apart and its limbs scattered; there was no blood, but Parric's mind provided it. Unwilling to cross the room, he stumbled out the front and, using the building for support, made his way to the backyard. Two more in equal sets of destruction, and the body of a man. His face was unrecognizable, his arms missing, and when Parric heard distant crashing in the woods beyond, he fled, waving his arms in front of him as though trying to brush away what he had seen like a spider's web that clung to his face.

Ike needed no further urging than the look on Parric's face to set the landcar in motion, almost leaving before Parric had closed the door. No one spoke to him until the road had unraveled a kilometer behind them.

Then, "What?"

"Jess," he said, "you wouldn't believe it." He closed his eyes, opened them quickly. "All the androids, at least I think it was all, pulled apart like they were made of paper."

"Did you check around the barrier?"

"No." Flatly.

"I don't blame you," Ike said, grunting to keep the car on the road and wind it to its highest possible speed.

"Was there a . . . a doctor?" Peg asked and, when Parric looked at her, said, "They told me about you when you were gone."

He tried to smile, knew it flashed crooked. "We never expected anything like this. Not in a hundred years. And yes, there was a doctor." He waited, sighed gratefully when he wasn't asked to elaborate. A man killed, androids destroyed, and it was obvious none was done by a human. It's possible they destroyed each other, but then, he thought, who had dismembered the last android?

"There was something coming in the woods. That's what got me running or I would have stopped to get some food."

"Forget it," Ike said. "I'm not all that hungry. I suppose I'm too fat anyway."

"Lose any more," Jess said, "and your camera'll be bigger than you."

Ike made a noise that might have been a laugh.

"What was it in the woods, Frank?"

"Don't know, Jess."

"That's the second time, third if you count the car being pushed out of its hiding place."

"Third time for what?" Ike and Peg asked simultaneously, and Jessica explained about the noise Parric had heard the night before.

"Are we being followed?" Peg asked, the intensely frightened look ghosting her face once again.

"I don't think so," Parric said quickly. "We're in this car, remember? If we're being followed, it would have to be on foot, and no one can travel that fast."

"You ever try running from a riot?" Ike said, then

shook his head. "Forget it. And in case you haven't noticed, we've been climbing, not dropping. Deeper into the mountains. Hills. Foothills, Whatever they call them."

Parric shaded his eyes with one hand to see past the glare of a white sun that swung back and forth directly in front of them as the road edged along the erratic curve of the slopes. It was true, he realized when the humid haze veiling the horizon thinned to permit sight of the higher peaks, and he couldn't help feeling a palpable relief; the mountains were something he could look at and count upon being there whenever he needed them, stolidly erect between him and the terror that stalked even the daylight hours.

They stopped twice. The first alongside a shaded clearing to ease the cramps in their backs and legs. During the second stretch of riding, Parric squeezed himself into the back, allowing Peg to sit with Ike, who was driving slower now, barely reaching 30 kpm as the road roughened and oftentimes narrowed to the width of the car. Jessica spent most of the time watching where they had been, but the sense of immediate danger faded as they filled the small compartment with talk, summoning memories that had lost their meaning, forcing exclamations of delight at the scenery less appreciated than the dread of its shadows. Parric stared at the back of Lupozny's head, wanting an opportunity to assist, refusing to volunteer at the risk of angering him again. There was little physical fear involved, but a definite dismay at the continuing sniping at his confidence. He told himself he was imagining it, twisting Ike's words to suit his own depression, but he couldn't make himself believe it.

They passed through a deserted village. Stopping at

the far end, Lupozny shattered the seals of a fuel pump and filled the landcar to its capacity while Jessica and Peg broke into a nearby house to bring back pans of ovenwall food and news that a discovered comunit was as useless and dead as Parric's had been. They ate quickly, in silence, sitting on the ground with their backs to the main street. Trees pointed shadows like flattened lances, shifting as a nightwind crept in early to lift the dust and set leaves scratching across untended grass.

Where did they go? Parric wondered as he climbed back into the car, automatically resuming his seat behind Ike. Did they run before or after their inoculations? Perhaps they had reverted to savagery and had melted into the hills; perhaps ContiGov had led them away to a relocation center of sorts. He was considering the possibility of all of them having died when Peg pointed to the right, up a thinly covered hill.

"A house," she said.

Parric only shrugged while Jessica hunched her legs and spun around to see for herself.

"Hey, there's another," she said.

When he bent forward, Parric could see, more than halfway up, swiftly vanishing glimpses of low, flat-roofed homes. He blinked and rubbed his eyes to clear them of weariness, and knew he wasn't mistaken when he saw brief glinting moments of reflection that seemed suspended in the air.

"A Town," he said. "Ike, find a way up. That barrier is still good. We could stay the night if everything's clear."

Ike drove a kilometer further, then pulled off to the side, sqeezing the landcar into a flattened area barely its size. "Can't get up there in this," he said. "If we go, we have to leave it."

"But you said if you shut it down, you might—"

"—not be able to get it started, that's right. But the way I feel now, I'll take that chance."

The women agreed, and Parric had no choice but to listen to the unaccustomed silence as the whine receded and died. But once outside, he refused to climb until they had at least made an attempt to cover the car with brush and leaves.

"What for?" said Ike, already leaving. "We haven't seen anyone all damned day, for crying out loud."

"Somebody might take it, and we're not that close to McLeod yet."

Ike stopped, turned, and pointed. "Look. Dr. Parric, I don't know why you're so damned excited about getting to this guy, and right now I think maybe your mind's a little baked. What we should be doing is heading for a city where there's people, soldiers, anyone who can tell us what's going on. Do you realize the whole thing could be over now and we're running around like a . . . a . . . a I don't know what?"

"Ike," Jessica said, climbing to him, stopping when he backed angrily away. "Ike, for God's sake, you saw what happened to that Town back there, and the village."

"We're kilometers from nowhere, Jess, and the people around here would run if I said boo."

"McLeod could be in trouble," Parric said quietly.

"So what? I don't know him. Jess doesn't, and neither does Peg. He's probably like that poor bastard in the last place."

"Don't!" Parric said, his throat closing to prevent the words he was thinking from boiling like acid onto the road. "He may need us. Peg's a nurse. She could help."

"She could help a lot more in some city, Parric." He took another step away, then wheeled and began to climb. Jessica remained as she was until he called, and she followed.

"Go ahead," Parric said to Peg, who looked to him, confused. "I'll be up in a second. There's something I want to do."

She balked a moment more, then hurried to catch up with the others.

The landcar creaked as it settled into the cool air pushed by the wind, and he kicked at it once before grabbing handfuls of debris and scattering it over the roof. He worked rapidly, faster, until he was running with bushes yanked by their roots, throwing, arranging, nearly crying in frustration when the car refused to disappear. He imagined Ike's face set into the ground and crushed it with as big a rock as he could lift. He ran into the road, looked forward and back, his arms spread to catch whatever might come his way; and when he tired, he climbed, slowly and carelessly, no longer worrying that he might be heard.

"Hey!" And he looked up.

Jessica was standing in the now-familiar cleared area in from the barrier. Parric felt the hair on his arms lift and knew the Town's protection was still activated. A good sign, and he instantly regretted how childishly he'd acted, mutely thanking the women for not mentioning it or asking what had taken him so long.

"Come on, Frank," Peg said, coming partway down

to meet him, taking his arm and pulling. "Jess already let Ike in. We were waiting for you."

"Good, thanks," he said, and in a minute was standing at the end of a street that could have been his own except for the houses: they were burned out, on the right charred and splintered, on the left totally destroyed with only a few contorted beams standing. Planks and grotesquely convoluted lengths of metal were strewn on the lawns and tarmac. Parric's elation drained as he walked with the women, keeping well away from wreckage still smoldering.

"Where's Ike?" he said when they'd covered the four blocks, seeing the clinic the only building undamaged.

Jessica shrugged, was mirrored by Peg.

"All right, then," he said, "he's probably taking some damned pictures. For history. Let's get the bad news over with first," and he moved quickly up the walk to the clinic door, pushed and stepped inside. The building was empty even of its furniture, but he nodded, pleased, that someone had had the foresight to disable the diagunit.

"It's okay," he said, returning to the front door. "We'll look around and see if we can't scrounge something to use for mattresses and we can sleep in here tonight. I doubt we'll find any food, but we can try."

A shout brought him around in a circle. Ike was running out of a house a block away. "In there," he called, but held up his palms when they started toward him. "It must be like when Doc went into the other one," he said, deliberately shuddering, then grinning broadly at Parric. "Like a mess of toys in a madhouse. There must be nearly twenty of them."

119

Parric frowned. "Wait a minute. Twenty?"

"Maybe a few more, why?"

"My Town wasn't much bigger, and I had forty-seven."

"Missing," Peg said, standing closer to him. "Some of them must have gotten out."

"No, they didn't," Ike said and pointed behind them.

There were four, all males, standing shoulder to shoulder in the middle of the street just beyond the clinic. Their hair was gone, their clothes torn or singed off, leaving splotches of black on their skin. Their faces were blank, but Parric knew they were looking at him.

"Frank?" It was Peg, and he realized these were probably the first she had ever seen.

"Ike," he said without turning around, "there's some metal lying in the street. Kick something good-sized to me, and find a chunk for yourself." He heard a footstep. "And take it slow. Very."

To cover Lupozny's movements, he took a step forward toward the androids, scanning them for signs of weakness. But there was nothing external, aside from their nakedness, that gave him cause for hope. And without their hair and the humanoid characteristics animation gave them, they easily could have been Fabor, or Dorski, or even Willard Dix.

"Frank—"

"Shut up, Jess." He heard a scraping, felt something strike the back of his foot. Carefully he worked it around in front of him without looking down, praying it was at least sturdy enough to swing like a club. "All right," he said softly, "when I start talking, I want you women to move very carefully to the nearest barrier edge. If you have to, run, and for God's sake, don't come back."

"What about us?" Ike whispered, and Parric grinned.

"Two little Davids," he said.

"And people wonder why I'm gray before forty."

There was nothing but a subdued and swirling wind. It was getting dark, but Parric had seen the shattered globes of the streetlamps and knew there would be no light once the sun had gone.

"You," he said suddenly to the androids. "I require your presence in the clinic."

A wooden *pop* and a single spark fluttered before dying.

"I said, I require your presence at the clinic!"

The android on the right stirred.

"I need it now!"

The center pair began to walk forward, their arms loose at their sides, their feet like heavy shoes on the street. The first shuffled sideways toward the clinic, the last remained motionless.

Thirty paces separated them when Parric reached down to pick up a blackened, thick section of a pole; as he straightened, he motioned Ike to his side.

"Eyes and hips," he said, trying to wipe perspiration from his palm onto his trousers. "Anyplace else won't do a damned bit of good. Eyes first!" And he leaped to one side when the androids broke into a sprint, their arms outstretched, their hands grasping. Impaired! Parric thought buoyantly and swung the pole as hard as he could, striking the nearest android square across the chest and upsetting its balance. Parric's hand stung so badly he wanted to cry out, recovering in time to shatter the face of the one Ike had tripped up.

In silence.

Whirling.

The pair's survivor regained its feet and grabbed at Ike's wrist. Lupozny screamed over the crack of bone and, for the first time, one of the women screamed in turn. Parric watched, stunned, until the little man's agony broke through his haze and he jabbed frantically at the android's eyes, blinding it but not making it loosen its grip. Ike was on his knees, his weapon useless and dangling from his entrapped hand. The android fumbled with its other hand but Parric crushed it before shifting behind and swinging wildly at its hips, the casing of its most vital mechanisms. He felt the give of metal beneath the pseudoflesh, felt too the babbling of Ike's anguish. The android was moving and Parric had to dance away from its lashing feet. He tried to disable the other arm but too often came too close to hitting Ike. Again he launched the pole at the hips, nearly sobbing when he spotted the motionless android stir and come at him. The fourth he could not see.

And silence yet another time.

Ike limp in the android's grasp, unconscious and being dragged blindly away.

Peg and Jessica reached for whatever weapons they could find and began striking it, the jagged edges of metal and wood ripping into the skin. The android kicked at Ike's head, missing in its blindness, missing again when it used its crushed hand as a club to fend off the women.

Parric waited until the last moment before diving at the now running android's legs, spilling it, rolling to his feet and battering its face until he was sure it too could no longer see.

Jessica called out and he ran back to Ike, grabbing his arm and trying to pull it loose. The android stopped, kicked, and caught Peg on the thigh, knocking her sobbing to the ground. As Parric circled, hoping to crack the arm at the elbow, Jessica made a grab for its legs, screaming when she was kicked into Parric, the both of them entangling.

Then the android lifted Ike with its one good hand, began to spin until Lupozny was clear of the ground before letting go and thudding him against a tree.

Jessica, who had reached her feet first, made an animal-like snarl, and would have leaped upon the android if Parric hadn't grabbed her by the waist.

"To Ike," he said. "Get Peg and go to Ike." Then he pushed her away and hefted the pole as he staggered toward the blind creature that was stumbling over the debris in the street. One of its legs was stiff, the other barely functioning.

One more, Parric thought, if I could have just one more.

There were three, trapped in a darkened world their manmade sense could not adjust to, wandering, making sounds that resembled inhuman whimpers, one breaking into an anguished screech that immediately reminded Parric of the night his house exploded. Two circled in front of the clinic, their hands raised toward the sky. Parric came upon behind the one that had battled with Ike and swung, pushing his body into the metal that cracked against its hip and spun out of his hands. The android went to its knees and Parric, crying, kicked at its back, wishing for the scapel to tear at its insides. Heedless of the android's attempts to grab his legs, he picked up anything his hands would close upon and threw, stabbed, clawed, and raked until he could stand no longer and fell backward.

A choking, then, and he raised his head. The android

had fallen onto its face, was hunched and crawling like a broken grub.

"Frank, over here!"

He pushed himself to his feet, not at all sure he could stand, and allowed the weight of his torso to carry him in Jessica's direction where he slumped onto the ground next to Ike, whose head was cradled in her lap.

"What about the others?" Peg said, looking fearfully toward the clinic.

"They'll wait," he said. "What about Ike?"

"History," Ike said weakly, only his hair visible in the darkness.

"You got it," Parric said, was about to reach for a hand when he bent and saw Ike's eyes close, his chest stop heaving.

"Hell," Jessica said flatly.

While the androids whimpered at the waxing moon.

Chapter 9

With the needled jabs of scrapes and bruises splitting into his remorse, he watched as Jessica brushed back a darkly matted strand of hair from Ike's forehead and lifted from his belt the tricorder he hadn't used. Her breath caught on the jagged edge of anguish, would have torn into keening if Peg hadn't taken her by the shoulders and made her stand. Parric looked up and watched as they embraced, his thoughts running in search of a direction, focusing finally on the androids still weaving, seemingly drunkenly, in front of the clinic.

Standing, he dryly scrubbed his face and neck, knowing little time had passed, feeling years settle onto the hillside from the silver-gray glow of stars and moon. Too much, he thought, and picked up a severed charred beam. He walked down the street, his eyes seeing nothing but the demonic dance of the mechanisms he had once thought to equate with men; and in thinking, stopped, remembering on the crest of renewed energy, the fourth android, the one he had ordered into the clinic. Skirting the helpless pair, he angled toward the front, trying to see into the black windows, but other than wind and whimpering, there were no signs that he and the women had further company. Cautiously he tapped aside the door with the beam, listening again until he pushed off the wall and stepped inside, suddenly blinded by the lack of light, then seeing only the square of the back room window through the connecting passage. He slid his feet along the bare floor, half crouching in expectation, the beam lightly balanced in both palms.

And still he was alone.

The examination room was empty, and he was puzzled, refusing to allow himself to panic when he decided the android had only temporarily obeyed him. And immediately his body shouted protests against the beating it had taken, warning him he was mortal and not likely to win again.

Into the backyard, then, searching as he crossed the grass for shadows that moved against the wind. But once back on the main street, he relaxed and dragged his wooden weapon on the ground behind him.

"Frank?"

"It's all right, Peg, it's me," he said loudly, and saw his mistake when the two androids in front turned toward him. He stepped into a trot. "Where's Jess?"

"Here, Frank," Jessica said, and he saw Peg's outline split in two.

"Let's go," he said, beckoning. "We can't stay here." He pointed. "Those two will be wandering around all night looking for us."

"But what about—"

"Jess, we can't stay."

He took her arm and pulled, gently. Peg hurried

ahead of them, her arms outstretched until they bent suddenly at the elbows.

"Here," she said, and when Jessica only stood immobile, Parric fished in her breast pocket and pulled out the patchkey. Handing it to Peg, he turned to watch the androids, saw that the one he had brought to the ground was rounding the corner, still on its face, still hunching in a lopsided caterpillar crawl.

"Come on!" Peg said, and he vented his mourning frustration by heaving the beam toward them before stepping through the disturbance to catch Jessica as she began to fall. She was heavy, and his arms trembled as he lifted and carried her through the remaining screens. Peg watched him stagger awkwardly and helped him shift Jessica over his shoulder before they descended the slope to lie on the ground next to the landcar.

From faint to sleep, Jessica remained still, and Peg stretched out beside her while Parric roused himself to sit with his back against their vehicle. Above them, faintly, they could hear high-pitched calls rising from the Town.

"They miss us," he said, dropping his head to rest on arms he had folded across his knees.

"There were four, Frank."

"I know. I don't know where the other one went. Maybe it fell off a cliff."

"Frank, is that what they're like?"

"No," he said, surprised at himself. "As a matter of fact, they're not. They've become infected, and no one could have anticipated such a thing happening. Normally they're really quite likable. Most of them, anyway."

"You liked them better than people."

"Who told you a thing like that?" He looked up, trying to see her expression.

"Jess."

"Oh." He lowered his head again. "To be honest, I guess I did. But it wasn't so much I dislike people that I had no use for them."

"I don't believe that. You should have seen your face when Ike died, and when you were trying to help me back there."

"I wasn't all that much help, you know. Jess—"

"You were there, and you didn't try to hurt me." In the darkness her voice grew younger, and younger still, until he remembered, vaguely, a child he had once seen on a Phillayork walkway: he had been on the medium speed, obviously traveling alone, and he had talked to himself in a low, frightened voice. The adults around him smiled at one another, but none, including Parric, had offered to open a conversation with the boy. When Parric had stepped onto the slowdown, he had paused to watch the child, lost him when crowds shifted to vanish him as though he had never been.

"Are we going to be all right?"

Were you all right, small boy?

"Frank, are you awake?"

"Barely," he said, smiling to himself.

"I'm sorry."

"It's all right. Don't be."

"It's just that so much has been going on, I think I'm afraid to close my eyes. I might wake up and you two will be gone."

"Without you? Listen, the first time I saw you, back on the road, the first thing I thought was that this girl needs a good lesson in how to bathe properly. How, I wondered, had she managed to survive all this time looking like that, for crying out loud? Also, I have to admit, I knew someone would have to carry me when the stupid car breaks down. Despite my superhuman appearance, you see, I'm really just a nobody. Hey, are you listening to me?''

He pushed away from the car, saw that she had pressed herself against Jessica and was sleeping. All right, he said silently, I can take the hint. He returned to where he had been sitting and lay down by the wheel, cupping his hands behind his head and watching the sky's rotunda darken, lighten, and blind him with sunlight.

Peg and Jessica were already awake, waiting for him. When he groaned, sitting up in spite of the rods that had been jammed into his back and arms, they helped him to his feet, oddly silent, and he frowned. Peg was evidently much better after her night's rest. She had tried to reassemble her clothes into a semblance of decorum, having brushed away much of the clinging dirt and leaves though her elbows and knees were still stained a brown-green and her back was traced with black where she had fallen the night before. As he looked at the single-piece, once-white outfit while she swept his feeble camouflage from the land-car, he wondered if she had ever worn a skirt and then, unaccountably to himself, hoped Jess would forgive him the thought.

And Jessica, though asked, did not help her. She stood to one side, watching mutely. She was as ragged as the others, but her face echoed only her own grief. He remembered how soft it had been when first she arrived, saw now that it had hardened, incipient lines tracking from her mouth and eyes; there were purple-black discolorations blotching her cheeks and forehead, and dirt smeared where she had tried to rub it off. The tie in her hair had snapped, and each strand was a string. Her hands were clasped loosely in front of her, and she didn't move when he lifted them in his own.

"Jess," he said, "we have to go."

"We talked," she said, "while you were sleeping." Her voice, at least, had not changed from the zephyred whisper. "We decided . . . well, we thought about what . . ." She lifted her face briefly to the sun and would not meet his eyes. "We talked about what Ike had said, and about what you had said, and we think we should go to your friend."

Parric dropped her hands. "I could be wrong, you know. Ike might have been right, and everything's all right."

"Stop it!" she said, suddenly angry, and Parric recoiled at the prospect of a slap. "I'm tired and I don't want to make up my own mind anymore. Damn it, Frank, you're not a clerk anymore."

"You don't have to tell me that," he snapped, yanking a shard of cloth from his shirt and waving it in front of her face. "Would a clerk be dressed like a goddamned beggar? Would a clerk have to kill—yes, kill, dammit!—just so he could see the sun come up again? You're tired? What the hell about me, Jess? I've been beaten, clawed, starved, and God knows what else when I should be back in my safe and stupid office watching some idiotic unit speak parables to me in dumb percentages. It was Coates, that self-important, overblown son of a bitch, who did this to me. It wasn't my idea, and I'll tell you the reason why I'm not running to some miserable horror in a city." He turned, then, and glared at Peg, who had stopped her cleaning and was watching him wide-eyed. "You know what the *Alpha* is? It's a starship, little girl, and if I can't be on it, then goddamnit, I'm going to make damned sure there's something decent for it here when it gets back."

"I thought you didn't care." she said when he gulped for air for another spate.

"Who the hell said I didn't care? Now, are we going to stand around here all goddamn day or are we going to find McLeod and get ourselves out of this mess?"

Without waiting for an answer, and suddenly embarrassed at his own uncharacteristic outburst, he yanked up the passenger sidedoor and half-guided, half-shoved Jessica inside. Peg, claiming she was smaller, crawled unprotesting into the cramped back, less of a chore now than when there were two. Parric slammed the door down and took the driver's seat. He hesitated when he saw the ominous array of dials, then took a deep breath with a prayer for Ike's ignition setup and slipped his hands into the cuffs. He triggered the engine with a flick of a thumb, pushing with his body as the motor whined through a nonstart cycle before suddenly leveling its pitch and he could feel a pull against the brake.

"Amazing," he said, grinning as his fingers folded around the handgrips and his left foot released the emergency stop.

"Well, I'll be," he said when the landcar lurched onto the roadbed and jounced down the gentle slope. It took several minutes before he could admit confidence in handling the machine, several minutes more before he relaxed his stranglehold on the grips and could guide it without jerking.

"I'll tell you one thing," he said finally, looking to Jessica, who was trying and failing not to smile, "I'll take a hovercat any time."

"You had one?" Peg said. "I thought, from the way you talked, that clerks only took the walkways."

"Once," he said, no longer daring to take his eyes from the road when he nearly flattened a storm-bent birch. "When I saved free time for a few days off, I'd take it to the coast and ride the water."

"Oh," she said, sounding disappointed, "a small one."

"It was enough for me, little girl."

"And stop calling me little girl, Frank. I'm nearly twenty-five."

Parric smiled, broader and wincing at the pulled scratches on his face when Jessica broke her silence and laughed aloud, coasting to the brink of hysteria, hovering, then easing to show she had returned to him, though as what he couldn't yet be sure.

"How far?" Peg said when the sun had lifted to bake them.

"I'm not sure," he said. "Trying to picture that question mark over the road is hard, but I'm pretty sure we're not all that far away. The hard part will be knowing when to stop and move into the hills to find him."

"What's he like?"

"That's hard to say. He spends so much time trying to goad the Central into giving him a raise, sending him women, bothering them just for the hell of it raises a smokescreen you can't always tell when you've penetrated. We'd lunch once in a while—"

"You've been there?" Jessica stared at him.

"No, of course not. We'd lunch, that's all. It means we'd put up tables in front of the comunit and talk while we ate. The Central didn't much care for that because the Town's links were separated from normal channels and cost more to operate."

"Something's up ahead," Peg said, interrupting.

Parric tried to see through the veneer of dust on the windshield, but it was as if the world had been enveloped in a tan haze. Then, at the side of the road, he saw a large dark object. He slowed, and as they passed it, saw it was a man lying facedown, his clothes ripped down the back. His feet were bare, his skin baked and dry, and welted with black pustules.

"Plague," Peg said unnecessarily.

Parric needed no instructions to speed up, and a pair of shoes crumpled under the wheels before he had time to swerve. The trees, then, began to fall away at infrequent intervals, and shacks could be seen in the clearings. Several had been burned to the ground, most of the rest firegutted and leaning precariously. Ritual, Parric thought. Comes the plague, comes the fire. Too bad no one has learned to burn the wind.

And in slowing again, he watched his left as a pair of raw wood shanties came into view, joined together by an umbilical crude breezeway. There was a clothesline stretched from a window to a tree and several men's shirts hung upside down. Since Peg and Jessica were busily searching the opposite slope, he didn't bother to point out the legs he could see in the front door. There was a dog dead on the unkempt front lawn, still tied to a stake half-pulled from the earth.

"I saw something," Jessica said, pressing a finger against the glass to show Peg where she was looking.

"I think it was a man, running."

"It couldn't be, not here," Parric said. "There's too much concentration of plague."

They rounded a bend, dipped, and began to climb again when, at the top of the rise, two figures jumped into the middle of the road. They were carrying rifles and made no efforts to conceal at whom they were aiming. Parric's hands loosened on the grips, then tightened as he slapped a foot heavily on the accelerator. The landcar shuddered, skidded almost into a shallow ditch, found purchase, and charged. Jessica had already ducked below the line of the dash, Peg had crouched as far down as she could although her head was still visible above the flattened triangles of the front seats. Parric could do nothing but stare as the car whined toward the men. By their hesitation in firing, he thought them surprised he hadn't succumbed to their threat, and since they wore no uniforms of authority, he wasn't about to ask them how soon it was until the next rain. When they finally did fire, it was as they leaped into the ditch, both shots only piercing the sky.

Thank God for projectiles, he thought, having seen what a laser weapon could do to the flimsy metal his vehicle was encased in, and then realized he was worrying for nothing. The bulky laser rifles had not been very popular of late, and had been kept mainly in the hands of the military. Still, his pessimism cautioned, a man desirous or desperate enough . . .

As the car topped the rise, he saw a wide and table-flat plateau, heavily wooded. Through the trees he could see open fields not large but sufficient to sustain a family or two with a surplus to tantalize those whose greed for the organic transcended expense. The road, too, had smoothed, unpaved but hardened by constant traffic.

"Who were they?" Peg asked, being the first to shake off the shock of the blunted attack.

"Desperate," Jessica said. "Looking for credits or food, or just someone to get at. There's a town up ahead, Frank. Maybe they come from there."

If they did, he thought, then we're in worse trouble.

"No," he said when the first tiny house cornered into view, "no, they weren't."

"This place," Peg said a moment later. "I don't remember seeing it when we flew over."

There was a freshly painted sign identifying the town as Eisentor, the historic home of Noram's first Vice President.

"Historic," Jessica said bitterly. "Ike would have loved it."

Eisentor was dead.

Hovercats and landcars were parked in the streets, orderly except for two or three that had crashed into others. The lawns, sidewalks, dollhouse-tiny porches were littered with the corpses of animals and birds. Approaching the center, Parric was forced to reduce his speed to weave between grounded 'cats that had slammed into poles, storefronts, the tops and sides of landcars. He tried not to look into them, his eyes watering from the strain of staring straight ahead, but from one a hand protruded, another swallowed half the body of a woman, shadowed the head of a child. In front of one building, single-story like the others, a quenchcat was parked and around it the masked and black-banded bodies of half a dozen firefighters.

Moving clouds of flies.

Crawling rivers of gleaming dark insects.

And the stench.

Parric swallowed, trying not to gag, picking up speed as the jams lessened and there was room for him to move.

He looked down at the dash.

"We're low," he said grimly.

"Don't stop," Jessica said. "I don't care if we have to walk. Just don't stop."

He swerved to avoid a flame-eaten truck, circling a block to keep them from passing the remains of what looked like a street meeting complete with a forlorn banner that begged for salvation.

Stores dropping away to houses mostly gutted, their white colored gray.

To fields tall and fallow.

He pushed aside the window to clear the cabin of the scent of death.

When the road resumed a perceptible climb, he stopped and got out without saying a word. Holding his sides, he walked around the landcar, kicking at the metal, the tires, the stones he found loose on the shoulder. He breathed deeply, angrily, brushing away a hope that the air was still unpoisoned.

"The Cities," Jessica said when he returned.

"I can imagine," he said, adjusting the cuffs.

"Frank," Peg said, leaning over the seat, her eyes red-rimmed, "how much longer?"

"If I knew, I'd be the first to tell you. And when we leave the car—"

"Leave the car?"

He nodded, understanding how she felt about jettisoning their only concrete source of protection. "We'll have to. The one thing I do know is that McLeod won't be on the road. Besides, the choice is hardly ours. We're going to be out of fuel soon.''

He started off again, pushing the landcar until the antiquated vehicle actively fought his unsteady guidance. Jessica and Peg, after desultory comments about anything at all that would exorcise Eisentor's specter, fell into sporadic dozes that made him envious and feel more tired than he was. He shifted the drive to his right hand and pulled the left from its cuff to rub at his eyes. He was momentarily blinded, then, when he swept around a curve and saw, too late, the tree that had been felled across the road. He braked, using both hands to yank at the steering rod and the landcar whined into a skid, sliding off the road in seeming slow motion before coming to a battered rest near the base of the blockade. He heard Jessica swearing before he passed out.

Chapter 10

"No more," he mumbled. "Don't want anymore. No more."

Whirlwind lights, imploding nebulae, a dark star reaching to pry open his eyes. He was sitting up, knew by the hard press of metal against his back he was propped against the landcar. His chest felt crushingly smaller in aching stripes where the safety bands had gripped him before the moment of impact, and he imagined his knees were swollen as though his feet had been jammed up into them. His right hand was partially numb, was returning sensation in a flurry of bee stings, and his left fumbled to cover it. The fact that he wasn't dead surprised and somewhat angered him. It was, he was ready to believe, the least someone could do to keep him out of pain; Coates never did anything the easy way.

"He's awake, Jess."

The voice was unworried and, without a face to go with it, apparently unconcerned. A hand, feather soft and professionally caressing, brushed across his forehead with a breeze that persisted in signaling the advent of rain. It was nice in the dark in spite of the tiny suns, but the hand became insistent, dropping to his shoulder to push slightly. His head tipped to one side and, to keep the dizziness from churning his stomach, he opened his eyes, slitting them to keep the overcast glow from adding to his headache.

He was facing the way they had come and he could see the gashes in the road where he had skidded, digging into the darker earth beneath the surface. Jessica was sitting just beyond his outstretched legs, her arms folded across her upraised knees, her head resting upon them. Peg was kneeling beside him, and he smiled before trying to stand.

"No," she said, using the same gentle hand to keep him in his place. "We're not going anywhere. Relax until your lungs get themselves back into shape."

"How long?" he said as he tried a deep breath and gasped at the razors someone had slipped between his ribs. "And how did you know about this?" He placed a hand carefully against his chest and patted it over the front, looking for the holes that must have been there.

"I never had a 'cat, but my brother once had a landcar that slipped out of control in Bosford. I know how those bands feel. Worth it, though. At least you're still alive."

He rubbed at his sides, doubtful her prediction was entirely accurate. "How long?" he repeated.

"I don't know," she said. "Maybe an hour. I'm not much good without a watch."

Immediately reminded, he looked at his wrist and saw the shattered timepiece useless in its chromium band. He scowled, pulled it off, and tossed it over his shoulder. "Jess, how are you doing?"

Jessica raised her head, brushed back her hair, and

smiled, albeit ruefully. "I was sleeping when you decided to end it all. The bands had a hard time finding me. My head hurts a little."

"Mild concussion," Peg said when he looked to her. "No problem except that she should be in bed with a mediunit nearby. We should all be there, for that matter, but what can you do, right?"

"What about you?"

"My shoulder got banged up when the seat hit it, that's all. Frank—" She turned to Jessica, who only shrugged, abdicating a responsibility Parric couldn't yet fathom. "Frank, I think . . . that is, we think it was deliberate."

He nodded and pushed to sit straighter. "I sort of gathered that. But it couldn't have been for an ambush or we would have been attacked by now. Or have we?"

"No, no, nothing like that, Frank. I meant, I think we were supposed to stop here, and whoever wanted that had to be sure we wouldn't pass this particular spot."

"All right, nurse," he said, "and how did you figure that out?"

He realized then that he had spoken too harshly when she looked slightly hurt and retreated to sit next to Jessica, who was rocking slowly, one hand carefully massaging the back of her neck. He shifted again, found breathing decidedly less painful, and shook his head.

"Sorry, Peg," he said. "I didn't mean to snap like that. Now what makes you think that tree is a signal of some kind?"

She pointed mutely toward one end, obviously still feeling the sting of his sarcasm. And where do you get off talking to her like that? he demanded of himself.

You're no more country than she is. He stared, trying to see through the remnants of his dizziness what she was trying to show him. Failing that, he pulled his legs to him and, with one hand pressed against the cooling car, got to his feet. He waited for a warning about his health, received none, and sighed loudly, hopefully sounding humiliatingly contrite.

The landcar was broadside to the lower portion of the brown-skinned trunk, crumpled and clearly no longer functional. The left front tire had been twisted parallel to the ground, the left rear battered off its axle by a stout stubby branch. Parric leaned heavily against the fallen tree, unable to control the spasm of trembling as he suddenly understood how close he had come to being killed. There was a second limb barely clearing the car's roof; had it been a handsbreadth lower, or had the car jumped before it struck, he would have been missing most of his head and torso, and so would Jessica.

As he pushed his hands against the bark, lowering his head to combat the urge to retch, the shaking subsided, but not the black pit fear that he was too mortal, too human to undergo much more punishment. And yet, absolutely against his will, there were the two women; that Jessica would be able to handle herself—she had to be or she wouldn't have survived her profession—that Peg would see her way through to whatever end, he had no doubts, but he bristled at the way they continually leaned on him. Somehow it wasn't the same category of responsibility he had assumed in the name of the *Alpha*—this was too personal for comfort.

Damn, but I'll be glad to see McLeod, he thought, and let him hold the cup for a change.

After examining the landcar's damage, he turned his attention to the tree itself. It took a moment before he understood it had been snapped instead of cut and had been dragged across the road. It was dead, as leafless as it had been during the winters of its youth, and where it had been torn from its roots was a mark obviously not made by the crash of the car: not large, and crudely fashioned, but an arrow nevertheless which pointed toward the slope on the right. He straddled the narrow trunk, looked down at the sign, and slowly followed its direction with his eyes, staring, puzzled, until he saw gashes large enough to be seen from the road in several more trees.

"Damn," he said. "Why the hell didn't they put up a sign? It would have saved me a splitting headache."

"How many people running away from a disaster would bother looking for an arrow carved into a tree trunk?" Jessica asked. She had risen, finally, and was standing beside him, trying to smile through the dishevelment of her hair and clothes. He grinned, pleased to see she was at last behaving like the woman he had known a hundred years ago. He swung his left leg back over the trunk and sat sidesaddle, his arms folded across his chest.

"I suppose you were the one who found this miracle," he said.

"Of course," she said. "I'm a reporter who's trained in looking for things other ordinary people miss." She looked back to Peg, who laughed. "Actually," she admitted, "it was luck. After we got you out of the car, I fell back against the tree, dizzy as hell, and when Peg tried to pick me up, I saw the mark. I didn't know what it was at first, probably didn't want to believe what my eyes were showing me. But when Peg saw it too, she wanted to follow the trail up the hill right away. I thought it would be better if we all went. It still might be a trap, you know. And it might not even be for us. It could have been here for days, maybe to keep those people from Eisentor from going someplace they weren't supposed to."

"Maybe," he said, idly brushing at some dirt on her sleeve. "But we'll never know unless we get moving. Of course, we could go on down the road, but my guess is we're as close to that question mark spot of Cam's as we'll ever be."

"Good," Peg said. "We might find us some shelter."

"All right," he said, standing when Jessica said nothing further. "I'd just as soon get into the trees, anyway. It looks too much like rain."

In a shift born of gloom, the sky had tinged itself a November gray laced with tendrils of twisting white, bottomed in glowering black. It coughed rushes of wind that felt wet even though precipitation had not yet begun, and the afternoon heat was replaced by a midnight chill.

Peg quickly joined them, testing against their halfhearted protests the various areas of most acute discomfort, insisting they couldn't get far if one couldn't walk on his own. Finally, she reluctantly decided there would be no further harm in starting out and, with a last spiteful kick at the wrinkled nose of the landcar, she led the way up the slope.

"I thought she was a mild little thing," Parric whispered as he brought up the rear.

"Never underestimate the power of a woman about to get soaked," Jessica said.

"Wisdom from an enigma," he answered, "and doubtful stuff at that."

When she refused to take the bantering bait, he kept

himself quiet and concentrated on finding ways to put his feet down without unnecessarily jarring what muscles he thought he had left. Unlike their first run through the country, they were being hindered by a profusion of thick and thorned underbrush that promoted frustrating delays, causing them to spend nearly as much time traveling parallel to the road as climbing toward the summit. Added to this were Peg's attempts to keep within the trail set by the marks gouged out of the bark, and Parric soon realized it would take them much longer than they had been silently hoping to arrive at a destination none would venture to speculate about. It began to seem ridiculously foolhardy to him, blindly following an equally blind trail. He wished they had not dismissed so handily the option of following the road. On the other hand, he thought in self-confusing bewilderment, unless McLeod has strung out a banner with detailed instructions, they could have just as easily fallen prey to another group of raiders, or another Eisentor.

He cursed, stumbling in the pressing darkness as they prepared for the sky to rupture, uncontrollably shivering whenever he was forced to step over or around the unnaturally bloated corpses of birds and small animals.

Jessica fell. He hurried to grab hold of her waist, but she twisted away, insisting she could take care of her own mistakes.

The land leveled and they moved more quickly.

The signs ended abruptly, but Peg would not stop. She continued to lead them as if her eyes could see things Parric could not. And yet he knew she was running away from and into desperation, not wanting to recognize that what they had had was now taken from them. By the time the rains fell, none had any notions left of returning to the road.

Moving then through two shades of silence: there were no animals, no birds, no insects to lighten the weight upon their ears; they would not, did not, speak more than grunting their assent to a new line of travel, their gasps swallowed, their curses stored for a moment when speech was no longer a luxury.

Moving then through two funnels of noise: the blood that drummed through the insides of their heads, the echoes of inner rasping breath water-laden and sea-drowning shallow; and the rainwind, awakening the trees to talk with one another in hisses of a pitfull of snakes, bending limbs to creak against limbs like the aging chatter of prehistoric insects.

And the rainwind itself, keening counterpoint to the black clouds' thunder.

Once the initial shock of cold water ceased its stinging, brought him numbing, Parric ignored the damp's forcing of involuntary shivering. Beneath the fallen leaves and patches of brown needles, the ground had become slippery and tended to shift under him whenever he looked up to see where he was going; and seeing was as difficult as the rain shattered itself into pebble-hard drops that looked like glass. His hands found it increasingly impossible to maintain a grasp on bushes and low-hanging branches; his eyes seemed closed more often than not. He fell more times than he bothered to count and coated himself in the forest's decay. Jessica dropped back to walk with him, then Peg, and they huddled against one another whenever space allowed, convincing themselves they were drier for it. In a wide, meadowed clearing they were shoved off their feet when the wind found them unprotected and pummeled them with buffeting fists; and once in the woods again, they stopped to rest as if they had discovered a broad-leaved shelter.

Parric wanted to tell them to forget about moving on until the storm had passed, but speech in the screaming dusk was useless, and he could only shrug when Peg poked him in the back and trudged away.

And when she began yelling it was several moments before he bothered to look up, at the backs of more than a dozen low houses all painted white.

Jessica stopped, her arms limp, unprotesting when he pulled her to him and kissed her hard on the mouth. Then she laughed, shook her head, and kissed him back.

Peg threw herself on them, tumbling them onto the ground, and they rolled like children in the night-cold mud before running to the clearing outside the barrier and looking down the center of the only street in Town.

"Patchkey," Parric yelled at Jessica. "Get out the key!"

Jessica fumbled through the pockets of her clothes, and he saw the tears pushing for room on her rainslicked face. He grabbed her shoulders and shook her, then slapped away her hands and tried his own search.

"Gone," he said to Peg, yelling above the wind. "We've lost the patchkey."

She stared uncomprehendingly at Jessica, took a step as if to slap her. Parric raised a hand but Peg had spun around and ran as close to the Town as the barrier would allow, her arms flailing as she tried to breach the invisible wall. Parric, too, felt like striking out, but the bitter dismay he saw in Jessica's face stalled him. Not knowing what else to do, he took her face in his hands and smiled. "Don't worry," he said, "We'll get in." He looked over toward Peg. "Watch her, and don't move away from this spot. I'll be back."

Jessica nodded dumbly and he ran along the course of the clearing, trying to see through the rain to the Town inside. It appeared to be undamaged, no signs of fire or fighting: and it appeared to be just as deserted. There were sidestreets, not much longer than his own Town's, and on one he saw a landcar. He stopped, leaning forward as if pure hope would create a living being within it. He ran further, slipping on the weeds and rain-flattened grass, slowing by what he assumed was the clinic, but the back windows were dark and he couldn't see through them. Turning around, he retraced his steps to the landcar and swerved into the woods where he hunted until he found a rotted fallen log. Grunting, struggling, he lifted it to his chest and carried it to the clearing where he gripped one end and began to turn in a circle until he felt the wood slipping through his hands. He flung it, saw it tumble into the barrier and fall to the ground as if slapped down from above. He found large rocks, as many as he could carry, and threw them, falling to his knees as he knocked himself off balance. If there was anyone within, the alarms would surely arouse them. But when nothing changed, he ran back to the front and explained to Jessica and a sobbing Peg what he wanted. It wasn't long, then, before they were pelting the Town with whatever could be lifted.

Once, pausing to keep his lungs from tearing themselves open, he looked down at his hands and saw the blood mixing pink with the rain. Hastily he wiped them against his shirt and reached down for a leg-thick limb Jessica had dragged to his feet. Dimly he heard the rise

147

and fall whoop of the sirens within the black casings, and beneath them the screaming imprecations of Peg's unconstrained madness. The combination of what struck him as two forms of equally mindless insanity made him open his hands and drop the branch. He straightened, took Jessica by the hand, and walked to the edge of the street. In front of him, Peg had slumped on her knees, looking up at him, through him, beyond to a place where, he thought, there must be peace, no storms, and no one that looked like him.

"Now what?" he said flatly, knowing there was nothing further they could do.

Jessica was silent, only tightened her grip on his hand.

"Are you sure you haven't got it?" He didn't know why he had asked, but there was always that chance that she could snap her fingers and pull a key out of the beaten air.

"Absolutely," she said. "What do you want me to do, strip naked to prove it?"

"I wasn't doubting you. I was just—" And he shrugged.

"Frank!"

Peg, having called, had twisted around and was pointing into the Town. Several blocks down Parric could see, faintly, the figure of a man edging cautiously toward them. The wind shifted to blind him temporarily, and he had to blink the water from his eyes before he could be sure he had seen the figure at all. Android? He dared not say the word aloud even though he could see it in Jessica's eyes. Peg apparently had not doubted because she was on her feet and shouting, jumping, throwing herself into a frenzied dance that quickly lost its momentum when she found herself alone in her elation.

"What's the matter?" she said, pushing at Parric. "Can't you see him?"

"I can see him," Parric said.

"Well?"

"*He* might be an *it*," Jessica said.

Peg shook her head. "No," she said. "That can't be."

Parric loosened his hold on Jessica's hand and stepped between them, past them to the limit of the barrier. He wiped at his face with his arm, pressed up against the outer screen, then turned around and grinned.

"Oh, damn," he said, "it's Cam McLeod."

He began calling, beckoning frantically. Only a block away, McLeod stepped out into the middle of the street, hunched over, then ran toward him, one hand diving into a pocket of his ungirdled tunic. There was laughter, unrestrained, and once the three were through the screen, a flurry of embraces, kisses, and an hysterical hilarity that continued unchecked as the stocky little man ran in front to lead them, ran back to pull them into the overwhelming warmth of his home.

"How?" McLeod wanted to know in a voice that scraped like wood against wood, and Parric, with a dozen diversions from Jessica and Peg, told him, at the same time watching as the Town guardian pounced from chair to chair in the living room, first sitting next to Peg, then by Jessica, but always keeping a darting eye on the angled front windows. He was completely bald, by choice rather than design, and his face seemed more rugged than Parric remembered, and more harried. There were folds of weight loss at his neck, and his left hand shook when he neglected to hold it in a fist or against his side.

"Wait a minute," he said finally, interrupting Peg's

account of how she had come to be with Parric. "You're dripping wet, for God's sweet breath! Through the kitchen and into the back room. There are some clothes there and a lav. Do something to yourself. You look terrible."

Peg laughed and obeyed immediately. Jessica, who had been almost rudely trying to assess the man through her experiences, moved more slowly. But when Parric rose, McLeod motioned him to retake his seat.

"The mouse," he said, not altogether unkindly, "had acquired a harem. Frank, I didn't think you had it in you, messing with all that lovely bare flesh hanging out like that."

"If I've got it, I've forgotten," Parric said, unaccountably annoyed. "I've been too busy running, in case you haven't noticed."

"May the Lord send him a lightning bolt with a hammer message, listen to the man!"

"You get religion since you came here, Cam?"

"That'll be the day. Just a few choice words I picked up from one of those white-robed missionaries that prowl these hills looking for what they can't get in the more godless cities." He paused, finally sat himself in a half-moon armchair Parric knew he had lifted from one of the android houses. Despite his often proclaimed awe for the apparent magic of the laboratory, he had also let it be known that there wasn't a man or android alive that was going to live better than he now that he had been given the chance. Parric had heard that promise a dozen times during their long-distance lunches and had often wondered just how poorly he had been living before Coates and the computer had admitted him into the group. Somehow, he had never found the opportunity to ask and, after the first few months,

150

decided it didn't matter; what did matter was that, for some reason incomprehensible to him, McLeod liked him.

"Cam," he said after a silence that required no words, "how are you doing?"

"Just fine," he said. "The Allah-Be has seen fit to protect me from all sorts of evils in this wicked, wicked world."

"Liar. What's the matter?"

McLeod fisted his hands and kneaded his scalp with his knuckles, and Parric noticed what it was that had been bothering him since the excitement had faded: Cam had not shaved, neither head nor face, and the black stubble that had erupted gave his features unneeded shadows.

"I'm lucky you found me," he finally admitted.

"How could we miss with that damned tree sticking through my car?"

"Tree? What tree are you talking about, Frank?"

"The one in the road, Cam," Parric said, suddenly tense.

"I haven't been on that miserable track since the war broke out. I think you'd better explain."

"No," Parric said, "you first."

Chapter 11

His Town, McLeod explained, was similar in designation and function to Parric's, the dual deviation being that it also included a store modeled after a ContiGov produce center, and a LottChance Parlor. His days were spent in the former playing the role of shopkeeper and watching the androids' reactions to the programmed daily shortage or surplus crises; three or four nights a week were spent in the parlor looking for the appropriate emotional consequences of large and small losses and jackpots. His diagunit was kept in the store and had been brought out front to disrupt the façade only when Coates had informed him of the war's effects. Deactivation had been a relatively simple matter.

''But I should have guessed something was up when some of them started looking at me queerly. I thought at first it was some kind of filament breakdown because the Central had instituted a long series of bad luck streaks in the parlor, and they weren't having the good times they were used to. In fact, I lost a fair bundle myself and was going to hit old Floyd for a raise as soon as he condescended to speak to me again. He didn't often, you know. Thought it would be good for me to stay away from the rigors of the real world.''

''That you don't have to explain,'' Parric said, although he wouldn't admit he had not minded being left alone. ''When he broke the news to me was the first time I'd had words with him in several weeks. The day Lupozny and Jessica arrived.''

There was a faint thump, and Parric jerked his head around while McLeod laughed. ''The disposor, Frank. Has a bug in it, that's all. The ladies are making sure their clothes never see the light of day again.''

''Don't blame them,'' he said, looking at his own tatters. ''But what's the matter, Cam? You're stalling. What's the trouble? Androids?''

''One,'' McLeod said, standing to lean against the wall by the front window, almost as a second thought reaching up to dial the lighting that cast a soft white from the ceiling. ''He wouldn't answer my summons, I piled the others in the back of the store—softened earth beneath the Saviour's feet, can you imagine me parceling out hunks of tins and soysteak?—anyway, the others were easily taken care of, but this one, Eagle, never showed up. I hunted him all over the damned place. Took his apartment apart—he lived in sort of a rooming house—and spent the whole afternoon every damn place he could have conceivably crawled into. Funny thing was, he hadn't been outright crazy like the others, and I couldn't figure out what had happened to him. I decided to check the store again. Nothing, but it gave me a lead when I heard a mess of laughing next door. Sure enough, that baldheaded tin man was sitting at a table trying to beat himself at a card game I still haven't figured out.''

153

He stopped, then, and turned when Jessica and Peg reentered the room. They had found ill-fitting tunics in his room, and he winked appreciatively. The clothes were close to the length of a man's formal singlet, but short enough to expose their legs to midthigh. Jessica still wore her kneeboots and managed the unsettling effect without much embarrassment, but Peg had only her thick-soled lowcuts and she instantly provoked Parric's laughter when she tried to sit without revealing her waist.

"It isn't funny," she said indignantly, but he couldn't stop, didn't want to, the feeling of good humor so recently alien. Finally she stretched out on the floor, her head propped on a bridge of fingers. "Stop staring and go on," she ordered when McLeod seemed too lost in his staring to remember how to talk.

He nodded, almost absently, and again watched the rain slap against the forest outside the Town. Some of the deluge passed through the barrier in a fine shower and occasional explosions of wind, and there was little more than the air-splitting lightning to measure the severity of the storm.

"I tried again to get Eagle to come along with me, but he wouldn't leave his stupid game. You don't know how I was tempted to twist that smirking head off his shoulders, but instead I wheeled the unit to him since he wasn't about to go to it. I set it up behind him, and he ignored me and everything else until I started to open his shirt. It must have been premonition or something, but I stepped back just as he swung an arm around and caught the unit right across its middle. I never saw so many sparks in my life! I just stood there, gaping, while he turned around again and played on like I wasn't even there. That's when I decided to leave him be."

"You mean he's still over there?" Jessica said, her hands fumbling for a time at her waist until she realized she was no longer carrying recorders. Parric wanted to ask what had happened to the one she had taken from Ike, but decided against it when her expression became momentarily confused and she looked as if she were going to cry.

"No," McLeod said. "That was day before yesterday. In the afternoon I went back to see if I could talk to him and he started throwing chairs." He took hold of his left arm and rubbed it. "Caught a piece of one and got the hell out. We've been stalking each other ever since, though he's never tried once to get in here. I had hoped there might be some residual obedience left, but after Frank here told me what happened to his babies, I just don't know. Maybe he's playing."

"Another game," Peg muttered.

McLeod took a swipe at dollops of moisture forming inside the pane and returned to his chair, throwing an abnormally heavy leg over one arm. Parric could see the chair shuddering in an attempt to conform to the awkward position and wondered if there was such a thing as deep-seated furniture neurosis. He laughed suddenly, then covered it with a cough when McLeod stared at him.

"Just thought of a bad joke," he said. "I wasn't laughing at you."

"You must be affected by all this," McLeod said. "You never made a joke in your life."

"Listen, Cameron—" Jessica said.

"Cam," McLeod corrected. "My friends call me Cam."

"All right," she said, smiling, "Cam. Does your comunit work?"

"Not since yesterday morning. The last thing I saw were the doles."

" Come again?" Parric said.

"Doles. Seems the ordinary lines of production, not to mention communication, have just about collapsed. Old Floyd was obviously understating the damage. Fires all over the place. Philayork, Lafrisco, even Descago seems to have splintered. God bless the earthworm, but it's like the whole country has divided itself into little half-baked kingdoms, those that have people left, that is, I suppose you saw Eisentor."

"Graphically," Parric said.

"They had a transmitter going for a while, looking for some help. Didn't do much good, I guess. Not even the Guard seems on the ball. In fact, the only soldiers I did see were standing in line like everyone else."

"Well, where is ContiGov?" Peg said, shifting to sit cross-legged after pulling a cushion from a couch.

McLeod scratched at his chest and raised his eyebrows in a shrug. "From what I could tell, it's moved to Kanaska, or maybe the Dakota Line, wherever that secret center is of theirs. Apparently trying to keep the big deals out of the plague zone. I doubt, though, that there's such a place left in the world."

"You said doles," Parric prompted.

"Oh, yeah, some of the governors looked like they were more on top of things than most. Some grabbed what they had left of a ContiGuard and sectorized most of the food processors. There were copters all over the place dropping parcels onto rooftops. Damnedest thing you ever saw."

"Ugly," Jessica said.

McLeod agreed. "That's exactly the word: ugly.

And as far as I can tell, before the comunit blinked out, we're in a relatively stable position compared to, say, Eurecom and some of the others. If the Gov will only get settled and come out of hiding, maybe things will get normalized soon.''

"Assuming there's anything left of the Cabinet or Executive," Parric said.

"Cheerful, isn't he?" said Jessica.

"He's probably right, though," McLeod said. "It's been a week, and all I've seen is a medicopt buzzing around.''

"Me," Peg said unenthusiastically. "It was probably my team."

A lull, then, punctuated by the frustrated grinding of McLeod's chair, and Parric soon excused himself to change out of his useless clothes. The kitchen, he noted in passing, was similar to his except for the organistove shoved into a corner, another trophy of an android house. In the bedroom, however, he immediately felt out of place. Where his was spartan to an extreme, McLeod had seen to it, no doubt through incessant wheedling, that there weren't any boudoir luxuries left that he didn't have. The bed itself took up most of the space, torn from its wall closet and lifted on blocks of wood. It looked large enough to hold all of them comfortably, and he couldn't help thinking what delights there might be in that possibility. And why not? he thought as he stripped off his shirt and rummaged through the wardrobe, if the world's going to hell, why shouldn't we enjoy ourselves?

Disgusted that his friend seemed smitten with exotic colorations and was infatuated with the most loosely fitting tunics, he chose the most drab and tucked it into his trousers, thinking he would rather have the damp muddied pants on in case he should have to run the woods again.

Vanity, he told himself. You just don't want Jess to see your legs.

In the living room he smiled at Jess' look of relief at his return, and listened as Peg finished telling McLeod about the tree and the fear that they might have been followed.

"It's not impossible," McLeod said when Parric detailed the noises he had heard the first night out and while he was in the Town by the bridge. "Your com-unit obviously went before mine, and I've been in, well, sporadic contact with some of the others. A few of the fools panicked when they got Coates' warning and let their barriers down to run before they finished deactivation."

"Renegade androids," Peg said, clutching the cushion tightly to her chest. "I think I need a drink."

"No," McLeod said. "I tore out the damned barcab months ago. Found it too easy to get drunk. What you really need is some syntabac to calm you down."

"No, thanks," she said as he reached for a compartment in the chair's arm. "That's bad for my nerves."

"And this mess is good?" But when the others declined, too, he shrugged and looked at Parric. "So, Frankie, here we are, and what are we going to do about it?"

"Sleep," Jessica said. "We haven't had a decent night's rest since we left."

"Not yet," Parric said. "We've got to know what we're going to do first."

"Seems to me I've been through this before," she said, grinning; then, to McLeod, "He and Ike, they could never agree on what to do next. Frank always won, but I could never figure out how he did it."

"Ike was a good man, Jess," Parric said. "I was just lucky, that's all. It could easily have gone the other way, you know."

"Well, I vote we stay right here," Peg said. "We've got company, food, a barrier that still works, and we're safe from those . . . men outside. I don't see any point in going anywhere else. Besides, where else can we go?"

"The cities are out," McLeod said, "and most of the countryside is either dead or off limits by virtue of local militia. The girl makes sense, Frank."

"The android," Parric warned.

"Between the four of us, I think we can handle him. Thanks to you, I'm not as worried as I was." He laughed, forced and without mirth. "I think I let myself get a little too soft around the flab."

"What did you do before you came here, Cam?" Peg said, and Parric suddenly felt as if a ritual screen had been shattered; but McLeod didn't seem to mind, smiling instead and leaving the chair to sit on the floor in front of her.

"If the truth be known, and I didn't even tell Frankie, I was, if you'll pardon the expression, incarcerated for a certain period of years."

"Jail?" Jessica said, too loudly.

"Rehabilitation, they called it," he said without looking at her. "I used to work for a subunit of Descago, adding budget figures and trying to figure out where the graft went. I cheated once on my ration credit, didn't get caught, and figured I could easily eat better than the next sap. Trouble was, I did get caught and spent the next couple of years listening to whitecoats telling me what a bad boy I was, how I was

159

too smart to do such a thing, and I would have gone out of my mind agreeing with them if I hadn't had the stroke of luck that got me in here. Coates thought I was redeemable." He grinned and laughed, this time sincerely. "If he only knew what I've done to this place."

"He knew," Jessica said, and added quickly, "I got a rundown of the whole operation before I showed up at Frank's. He mentioned you two as being the most reliable, and the most unstable, of the lot."

"Unstable?" Parric wasn't sure, coming from Coates, whether or not that was an insult.

Jessica shrugged. "Whatever," she said.

"I think I've been had," McLeod said, would have said more but something thudded heavily against the porch and bounced harmlessly off the windowpane.

Peg yelped and Jessica fell to the floor, one arm flung over the nurse's back to keep her down. Another thud and McLeod had dimmed off the lighting while Parric ran for the front door, waiting for him before opening it slowly.

Though the wind had increased, the rain had stopped, and Parric squinted in order to see clearly. In the uncannily familiar setting of houses, streetlamps, and slickened road, he could see nothing but crab-crawling leaves racing one another in the gutters. The shadows were deep, and the lack of additional light from the other houses strengthened them, but as soon as his eyes had adjusted sufficiently, he moved to the top of the steps and grabbed the supporting post. McLeod stood beside him.

"You always ease the barrier when there's a storm?"

"Sure. Didn't you?"

"I always used the ClimatCon."

160

"You always were soft, Frankie."

"Pal," Parric said and descended to the front lawn, the muscles in his legs and across his back tensed to spin him around should the attack continue.

And still there was nothing but the wind.

"Cam," he said, bending, "if this is your boy—"

"Who else?"

"—then he's about to break loose. We might as well stop it here if we can or we'll never get any rest. And I didn't come this far just to get myself killed."

They returned to the house where McLeod despaired at finding weapons heavy enough until Parric pointed out the gently tapering blue metal of the kitchen table's legs. McLeod protested feebly, Parric insisted, and McLeod fetched a toolkit to unbolt the gleaming, stem-like bars. Jessica wanted to be with them, but Peg declared she had had enough of night battles with robots and didn't want to stay alone in the house.

"Stick around, Jess," Parric said. "There's no sense in the four of us getting our heads knocked off."

"That's what I like about you," she said as she walked with him to the door. "Full of the old confidence."

On the porch, he and McLeod hesitated until postponement was impossible, then walked side by side down the steps, turning right and crossing the lawn. They had intended to use the grass to muffle their walking, but the rain had softened the dirt and they noticed immediately the sidewalk would be more silent. At the first corner, then, McLeod, through hand signals and facial contortions that almost made Parric laugh, indicated that he would patrol the backyards and hopefully they could time their progress to check on each other at successive intersections. Parric nodded, watched as his friend disappeared into the darkness.

Alone, again, and waiting.

He held the blue leg loosely in his left hand, the right frequently brushing over his face and hair at cobwebs the wind seemed to cast over him. He imagined himself in a corridor of the *Alpha*, strolling to the bridge to bid greetings to the captain, and he was saddened when he could not remember the man's name.

He thought himself on a Philayork street, the houses extending themselves into the grimly lighted sky and buzzing with the lives of people turned drones.

He was the emperor of a fanciful country, traveling incognito to observe the melancholy of his subjects and touch them with wands of hope and dreams of starbright futures.

He arrived before McLeod at their first checkpoint and waited impatiently until the little man paused at the edge of a light and waved shortly.

He was late at the second, saw McLeod pacing nervously until he was noticed.

The third, and the fourth, and finally at the fifth where he turned around, deciding it was a waste of time and entirely too dangerous. He told himself he should have known better and was anxious for Cam to join him.

There was a shout, and McLeod raced from behind a house halfway up the block, grabbing onto a tree and holding to keep himself from slumping. His hands were empty.

Parric ran up to him, held his shoulders until he could stand without aid. There was a dark streak across his forehead that came away damp when Parric reached out a finger to trace it; and over his shoulder he saw the android advancing, its right arm hanging uselessly at its side. McLeod stumbled away as Parric stepped back into the street, knowing it would be futile to look for some dark corner, knowing the android would see him no matter where he went. He lifted the metal club, saw the android hesitate before resuming its steady, unhampered walk. Its feet made slurping noises in the mud and, when it stepped onto the sidewalk, the curb, the street, he saw it was bald.

When they were separated by a bare two meters, McLeod shouted and it turned. Parric instantly lunged, striking at one eye, hearing the lens shatter as he danced away and shook the numbness out of his arm. McLeod shouted again, and Parric darted forward, slipping this time and losing his grip on the club. On hands and knees he scrambled clear, imagining the hum of air as the android's hand swept past his ankle. A third shout, this one different, and Parric looked up, saw McLeod pointing and turned around. There were two of them now, and Parric was confused, too startled to move when the newcomer grabbed McLeod's berserker and wrestled it to the ground. He thought of Fabor and Dorski in their silent fatal struggle, and watched it happen again as the two androids, in darkness unrecognizable, clenched at each other's middle seeking the vulnerability of their hips' powered source.

"Who—"

Parric waved McLeod silent.

The second android was bent backward, lifting an arm to press against the other's throat. There was a moment's statue immobility before a snap made the two men jump, and the first android's head dangled by threads of its synthetic flesh. Parric felt his lungs ache with air he could not release, and his arm began to sting where McLeod was punching it in his excitement.

163

Suddenly, the second attacker stepped back, whipped out a foot, and brought the other to its knees. It pounced, and a few seconds more sounded the crack Parric knew meant death. With sparkling metal catching the light of the streetlamps, Eagle lay motionless, and the second android pushed itself to its feet.

McLeod, shaking off the hypnotic effect of the struggle, grabbed at Parric's club, but he was pushed away when Parric walked to the fallen simulacrum and looked into the shadow. Then he held out his hand and the patchkey he had lost a hundred years before was dropped into his palm. As his fingers caressed the cool triangle, he prayed for the right answer to what was now only a sense of things returned to normal.

"Damn it, you took long enough, old man," he said. "Can't you do anything right?"

Willard Dix, shambling into the light, ducked his head in apology. "I'm an old man, doc. I can't move as fast as I used to."

Parric tried not to sag, forced himself to ignore the chance he had just taken. He smiled as McLeod finally came to his side, his face white, his eyes blinking rapidly. "Goddamnit, Frank, who is this?"

"Name's Will Dix. Comes from my Town."

McLeod immediately took several paces backward. "Wait a minute! For the Light of Buddha's eyes, you mean he's an android?"

Parric nodded, tossing away the table leg and laughing when McLeod took a step toward it. "Relax, Cam, he won't hurt you. Will you, old man?"

"Not unless he doesn't like my singing," Dix said. "Doc, I've been following you all over the place. Why wouldn't you wait for me?"

Parric took the android by the arm and began leading

him back to the house. "Will, I just didn't know it was you. It was damn frightening out there, and I didn't want to bump into anyone unfriendly."

"I want to know what's going on around here," McLeod said.

"You told me you needed me," Will said, his stance resuming its characteristic slump, his walk its unhurried amble. "Of course, I was sick for a while, but you should have stuck around and maybe I wouldn't have had to run through those miserable trees. Lots of bad things out there, doc. Don't know how you managed to take care of yourself."

"I have a feeling I had an angel."

"Well, I couldn't just pop out a couple of times. You might have done me like you did those others."

"I guess I did do all right, didn't I?"

"Frankie, curse the eyes in your head . . ."

Parric stopped and pointed to him. "Will, this is Cam McLeod, the guy I was going to send you to if you didn't behave."

McLeod kept a wary pace back even though he nodded and cast a short wave.

"Little," Will said sourly, "but not like the other one."

"Ike," Parric said.

"Him. Jumped around too much, that one. Always trying to take my picture."

"He's dead, Will."

"Know it. From a bad one like that." And he turned his head to look briefly behind him.

"Lots of them," Parric said.

"How do we know he's not one of them?" McLeod demanded.

"I was sick once," Will said, as if that explained

everything. "Someone's coming."

Parric and McLeod tensed, then relaxed as quickly when they saw Peg and Jessica coming down from the porch. Peg was holding tightly to Jessica's arm, trying to stay behind her as she stared at the android; but Jessica, when she recognized him, broke away and ran up to hug him. Dix did not respond, looked down only and waited until she had backed away.

"Oh," he said. "The pretty one."

"Oh, the pretty one," she mimicked. "Where the hell have you been, Willard Dix? Thanks to you, I've had to put up with Parric all by myself."

"Pity," the android said.

Parric watched as they traded insults directed primarily at him, and then yielded to the tugging of McLeod's hand. They stood off to one side where Parric explained how Dix had fit into the scheme of the Town. "And it looks like he's been waiting for a chance to show himself where we wouldn't kill him, too."

McLeod looked doubtful, both hands scrubbing at his face and scalp hard enough to make Parric think he'd rub off his skin.

"Relax," he finally advised, watching as Jessica introduced Will to Peg, grinning at the laconic answers to the nurse's machine-gun questions. "We've got nothing to worry about. Obviously his malfunctions weren't permanently disabling. And face it, Cam, if we get into more trouble, we could use him."

"I suppose," he said reluctantly, "but you'll have to excuse me if I heed the warning of the Prophet and am not overly friendly in his company. I'm beginning to get paranoiac about people with strange insides."

"Look," he said, laughing, realizing he was again

soaked to the skin as the storm crested a second wave, "we'll talk more in the morning. Right now, if you don't mind, I think I'll get me some sleep."

"I thought you wanted to decide what to do next?"

"God Almighty, Cam, you sound like Jess. And, if you must know, I've already made up my mind, but I need some time to be sure I'm not streaking off in a thousand different directions. And," he added before McLeod could pursue the hints, "I also feel more safe now than I have in days. I'm tired, Cam, and damn but I need the rest."

McLeod opened his mouth, then raised his arms in an elaborate gesture of resignation. He was, he said, going to suggest that the four of them might find it more comfortable in his own little bed, but if Parric was going to spoil his plans, as he always had, he wasn't about to argue. Not this time.

"Just give me a couple of chairs face to face," Parric said, "and believe me, the way I feel now, I won't know the difference."

Chapter 12

"It seems pretty clear to me what has to be done," he said to McLeod. "If we're going to help people like those poor saps in Oraton, I just can't see any other way."

It was midafternoon, and they were sitting on the top step of the LottChance Parlor. The storm had finally spent itself against the sides of the mountains and only shards of gray-turning-white clouds remained. The sunlight was fragmented, sweeping by in minute-long waves, and the heat had returned to dry the streets and make Parric wonder if the chill of the rain had been as bad as his nightmares remembered; yet, despite the frequent terror of those disturbing dreams, he had slept well, slept long, and when he had awakened shortly past noon, he was the first one in the kitchen. Not wishing, then, to play the thief to the others' recuperation, he walked for an hour, looking for sense in the dead charade, examining the natural and manufactured landscape for a supranatural augury that would take the burden of decision from him. He rummaged through several of the deserted houses until he found clothes the proper size and, with only slight qualms about being the first human to wear them, donned tan trousers and a billowed matching shirt. Feeling comfortable for the first time in times unknown, he stepped outside and saw Cam waiting for him at the parlor.

No escape in omen hunting now, he had thought, and crossed the streets to tell McLeod what he had concluded.

"The sentiment is fine, Frank, and I couldn't agree with you more, but do you really think it's the right thing to do now? I mean, here we're safe and all we have to do is wait until things get straightened out. And if they don't . . ." and he shrugged. "Well, at least we'll die happy."

Parric, leaning on his forearms, didn't look away from the tree he had been staring at. "You don't believe that any more than I do, Cam. Things are different now, things have changed."

"Not as much as you have, Frank, and to tell you the truth, I don't know what to make of it."

Parric wanted to say he didn't really care now that he had made up his mind, but chose instead to reach down to flick a damp blade of grass from his shoe.

"Cam, it's the only way we can go without cheating. The way I see it, people are going to need help, and they're going to need it in a hurry. With so many dead, God knows how many dying, nothing is ever going to be the same again, at least not for a damn long time. If we're lucky, we can stall off another war until people get smart."

"Now you're dreaming, old pal. That way has been tried a million times before."

"So we try it again. Look, it's simple, really: as soon as we're ready, we'll head for the Central. It's a complete, absolutely complete Town in itself. Coates, if you'll remember, lectured long and hard about that aspect of the Project. All that our little places were is contained in that one huge complex. It has total facilities for repair, maintenance, even a shop to build new androids just like old Willard. If we work at it, get it going without a hitch or a halt, we'll be able to do some judicious restocking in communities that need it the most. The Cities, Cam, the organifarms and the factories. There's too much work to do and too little numbers. If we want to stop a slip and slide into something worse than prehistoric cave dwelling, we've got to do it.''

''And what if those poor little people you want to help so much don't want you near them? In case you've forgotten, those friendly cavemen from Oraton didn't think a hell of a lot of you.''

Parric stabbed at his knee with a finger. ''That,'' he said, ''is where Coates and people like Jess come in. The name of the phase will be reeducation. Listen, Cam, our survival depends on it. We can't afford this dimwitted, shortsighted, practically superstitious fear of androids. For crying out loud, if we can't handle that, what the hell are we going to do if the *Alpha* actually comes across an alien civilization? Are we going to throw it back into space and forget about it?''

''Most likely,'' McLeod said. ''Or build a warship and blow it all up.''

''Now you know what I'm talking about!''

''Hey, listen, old friend, I've known what you've been talking about for the past two hours, and my ears are killing me. My point is, if there's all that doubt about success, why bother? Why give up our own little heaven for what might be a bigger hell?''

Parric stood and paced the length of the walk from the steps to the sidewalk. He knew he shouldn't allow anger to infiltrate his thinking, not now. McLeod was only voicing the same objections he himself had delivered during his own mental wrestling.

But it was so obvious. Perhaps, he doubted, too obvious. Perhaps he had blinded himself in the light of his own conception, a reformed cynic, a mid-thirties true believer.

And then, there was Eisentor.

And the doles.

And the riots.

And bloated masses of the dead.

"It may not even be there," McLeod said, stretching his arms over his head as if reaching for a ration of sunlight.

"Maybe not," Parric said.

"And what about that savior of yours, the old man?"

Parric frowned. "What about him? You owe him, you know."

"Yeah, maybe. But how can we trust him? Why the hell should he be the only sane machine left in the world?"

"Maybe he isn't," Parric said, "but—"

McLeod glared at his hands, then up to the sky. "But what? I don't like him, Frankie, I'll tell you that now. I've damn near been killed a dozen times, and I can't see that Dix is any different from the others. Quiet *now*, maybe, but the next time we sleep . . ." and he drew a finger across his throat in a too-graphic gesture.

Parric said nothing. This too had been integral to his doubts, and it was more a sense than illustration of logic that he believed Dix could be trusted. There had been a moment, a frighteningly long moment, when he'd been ashamed of his distrust, quickly suppressed it. If the android was functional, he would be invaluable not only in reaching the Central, but also in its own now uncertain future.

If he was functional.

I was sick once: deception, or a typically laconic explanation?

Sick once, sick again?

Damn, Parric thought, I can't start this all over. There would be no proof at hand at all, he realized—only in the traveling. A risk. And there was too much at stake not to grab it.

"He'll do as I ask," he said to McLeod's glowering impatience. "I'll do the watching."

"If you don't, I could be dead. And Jessica."

"He goes."

"I'll have to think about it," McLeod said, wandering off toward the house.

"Do that," Parric called after him, "but don't take as much time doing that as you do eating or we'll never get out of here."

"Doing what?"

Parric turned just as Jessica left the ContiGov store. Somewhere in the ranks of dun-colored dispensers she'd found a clothing unit which had given her an outfit exactly like his except for the color: a night-forest green that turned to solar fire the hair she combed with a slim-handled brush. The facial lines he'd noticed the day before had softened, blending into her equally soft features until they'd almost vanished with the events that had caused them. Suddenly he felt awkward, embarrassed, and boyish, and he took a rapid swipe at his own hair as she came up to him.

"You know," she said, looking around at the Town

as if seeing it for the first time, "I don't know why they built these places."

"What's the matter with them?"

"My clouds over the royal Coates' jowls," she said, grinning in mocking imitation of McLeod's impotent imprecations, "touchy, aren't you, doc?"

"Maybe, but what's wrong with them?"

She stepped down off the curb and pointed as she spoke. "Look at it, Frank, it's too unreal. I don't know what your dear supervisors were thinking of when they constructed it, but there's nothing right about it, nothing at all."

"I don't get it."

"Look again," she said. "The trees, all that lovely shrubbery and manicured lawn space. Fresh paint, trim houses, straight without a speck in the gutters. It's just rained and there's not even any mud on the sidewalks." She looked up at him, her expression expectant, but he could only stare back and feel uncomfortably stupid.

"It looks fine to me," he said finally. "Very pretty."

"Frank, for a man that's doing a pretty fair job as a part-time hero, you're not very bright." She grinned away the sting and took his hand, leading him across the street to the nearest house. "Too nice, Frank. I'm a reporter, right? I'm supposed to see things terribly profound in your daily life and tell you not only why they're profound, but also why they're there in the first place."

"All right, all right," he said, "so I'm not taking offense. Explain, will you?"

"Every little thing about this Town is false. You said you've spent most of your life traveling the walkways from home to office and back again. You've seen only

173

the Cities, and I'll bet not much more than Philayork. You were supposed to be training these androids to exist in a human society with a minimum of disruption. So why not put them in what human society is really like?''

"Hey, don't get mad at me. I didn't think this up."

"No, but you're going to have to, aren't you?"

He pulled her to her feet after she had knelt in front of a bush carefully trimmed to the right degree of shaggy, misshapen abandon. "What do you mean by that?"

"We reporters also snoop, Frank."

"You heard me arguing with Cam and you didn't come out?"

She shook her head and dodged a playful slap at her hips. "Most of what you said makes real sense," she said, backing away, "but you've got to do something about all this perfection. It just won't do."

He took a step, feinted a sprint, and laughed as she took refuge behind a tree. Laughing louder, he chased her until he realized he wasn't fast enough, and she was purposely allowing him to close in.

"Jess," he said, leaning against a corner lamppost, "maybe it is too perfect, and maybe the Central is just a bigger Town with all the faults you say it has, but we can't let it go just because of that."

"Who said we were going to let it go?"

"In fact, why couldn't we make something like this the norm instead of the ideal? With the androids' help, it might not be so farfetched. We could come close, anyway."

"Frank," she said, a hand on his arm just long enough to make him feel warm, "what happened to the *Alpha*?"

He scratched at his forehead, looked up at a crescent

of sun riding above a streamered cloud. "I don't know. It's still up there, I guess."

"You haven't forgotten what you said about it, have you?"

"No, but does it matter?"

She looked bemused. "A little," she said.

And they were quiet, saying nothing and knowing nothing needed to be said. The afternoon passed and they walked, not touching, and when his stomach decided it could no longer be put off by the confusion within him, she raced him back to the porch where she collided with Dix, who had just opened the front door.

"Hot to be running," he said.

"Working up an appetite," she said. "Where's Peg?"

"Inside. Watching the screen on the wall."

Parric darted past when he heard. Peg was sitting on the floor making soft suggestions to McLeod, who had taken the ornamental console panel off the outwardly slanting control unit and was elbow-deep inside it. She hushed him when Parric began a question, and he turned his attention to the screen. Where there had once been only filmy gray, colors now spattered; where there had been nothing but a suppressive silence there was the difficult to hear but unmistakable sound of garbled voices.

Parric refused to believe it, knelt beside Peg and gripped her shoulder as she directed McLeod with what she saw and heard.

"How?" he whispered when she stopped for a moment.

"I was sitting here trying to figure that old man . . . android . . ."

"Man is fine," he said impatiently, thinking Cam

175

had infected her with his doubts, "as long as you don't forget the other."

"Well, I was . . . shapes, Cam! Like ghosts behind all that static."

McLeod grunted, straightened to ease the strain on his back, then plunged in again.

"I was listening to him talking," she continued, "and . . . did you know he was the one who led those men away from you and Jess when you escaped your Town? Anyway, I was watching the comunit, just sort of imagining I could talk to people I used to know, when all of a sudden there were colors bouncing all over the place. At first I . . . the shapes are gone, Cam!"

"Bastard son of a preempted monk!" McLeod yelled, kicking at the baseboard.

"Back again!"

"Lord of sweet holiness," McLeod muttered without looking up.

"So?" Parric prodded.

"So nothing. I thought I was seeing things until the old man said something about his lenses going bad. Then I called Cam and he said he would try to boost something or other so that something else would do something right for a goddamn change." She grinned at Parric's startled expression. "That's a quote, by the way."

"I gathered," he said dryly. "Cam, is there anything I can do?"

"Yes," McLeod said, "but there are ladies present."

"Thanks," Jessica said, taking a seat behind Parric, smiling at Willard, who chose the couch.

"Light!" McLeod shouted, and Dix immediately

176

dialed the ceiling's glow to its maximum intensity. Parric blinked until his eyes adjusted, then repositioned himself to keep his reflection from disrupting the screen. The hope that contact with the rest of the country might soon be reestablished manifested itself in the sudden and prolonged silences that greeted McLeod's successive commentary on the ancestry of those who had fostered the comunit linkage. Cocoons of concentration were spun, manipulated, designed in prayers that elemental singlemindedness might prove to be concrete enough to drive the screen into life. Parric's eyes began to water, but he made no move to clear them, letting the tears fall onto his cheeks; he wanted nothing to disrupt the aura of possible salvation.

An hour, then two, and Jessica rose to disappear into the kitchen.

Dix became one with the furniture.

Jessica returned with cups steaming, placed one in front of each of them, but neither Peg nor Parric moved to pick them up.

Peg was whispering the progress, hissing the falling back in a continual atonal concerto to McLeod's violent percussion outbursts.

And in the background: voices, words, a phrase unintelligible but encouraging nevertheless. Then, for a full minute, a picture of a deserted Philayork walkway; a thirty-second scan of a makeshift barricade in a city unnamed. In order to utilize as much power as possible, McLeod bypassed dimentional depth modules and instantly there was the picture of a man standing in front of the Noram flag reading from a sheath of papers. Parric could not understand the speech, the words buried by static into what could have easily been an alien tongue; nor did he recognize the official, and he pounded his fists against his legs in frustration. It might have been a moment of reassurance for the populace, one that explained that all was well and the continuity of Noram existence had once again been fueled; but he doubted. The man was haggard, his infrequent glances at the camera self-conscious and uncertain. His lips kept pulling into shadows of smiles only to fight and return to tight irresolution.

"Come on," Parric whispered.

"I'm trying," McLeod said, breaking on the verge of tears.

A flashaway, then, and a compound filled with men and women dressed in nonentity gray, their faces sullenly angry, their movements physical definitions of defiance.

A soldier struggling with two guards as they dragged him toward a gleaming stake in the center of a concrete field; a firing squad at ease along a ragged white line.

Stores looted, burned, shattered by the force of a thousand grasping hands.

"Christ," Parric said.

A tapeclip of the President waving to a crowd obviously enjoying the best of times during his last campaign.

The speaker again, holding the papers at his side, staring dumbly at someone off-camera, fidgeting until fade to black, black to gray, and a newsroom with a world map shaded a deep pink.

"Forget the sound, Cam," Parric said finally. "We don't need it to know what's happened."

McLeod stepped back from the wall and stared at the screen, one hand absently caressing Peg's hair.

The reporter's face was grim and it was all McLeod

needed to see. He flicked off the trivid and no one complained.

"So," he said, "it looks like Frank gets his way again."

"I still don't want to go, now more than ever," Peg protested. "If that's what's going on out there, it's certainly safer where we are now."

"Perhaps," Parric said, "but for how long? Not that we'll come under any really sustained attacks, not with people too busy trying to add to the confusion. But how long can we stay here alone knowing there are probably others out there like us? I couldn't do it, Peg, I'm sorry. I can't stay. Definitely not."

"You're crazy," she said.

"You're young," he answered.

"Not all that much younger than you, Frank, but you're acting like an old man, for crying out loud. Who do you think you are, the savior of the world?"

"Peg!" Jessica said.

"Forget it," Parric said, standing. "No, little girl, I'm no savior of anyone's world, least of all mine. But I would think being a nurse would give you a reason to live, not a reason to bury yourself in a mountain grave."

"I'm not a healer," she said, quieter, less sure, nearly mouthing what Parric said next.

"Neither am I, but I can learn."

"You're both sounding like eulogists," McLeod said, pulling a syntabac packet from his pocket and stuffing it into a corner of his mouth. "Whether we go or stay, we're not about to change the world overnight. The question still in my mind, despite what I said before, is whether it's worth leaving."

"It is," Parric said simply. "And I'll be gone in the morning. You all can do what you like."

Leaving, then, he ignored the stares and an admonition from Dix to watch the night air. He leaned against the porch railing, thinking nothing, the thoughts too complex to sort themselves into coherent interior dialogue. Moods: nothing more, nothing less; and a hurricane's eye shrouded in disappointment.

"The clerk's crusade."

"Don't, Jess. I'm not in the mood."

"I was serious, you know."

"What are you looking for, a position as official camp follower?"

"Historian. That's what I was sent out here for, remember?"

"You have no equipment."

"Since when have I become deaf and blind?"

"Depends on how good your memory is."

"Good enough to remember you were scared to death of me that first day."

He laughed, shaking his head, and turned to hold her as Dix joined them.

"The girl's crying," he said. "Doesn't want to leave."

"She will," Jess said. "McLeod won't want to sit here doing nothing, either."

"And what about me?"

"What about you?" Parric said quietly, and Jessica's arm tightened around his waist.

The android stood in front of the window, the light behind turning his figure to shadow. "I was sick," he said. "I am well. They will want to know how."

And if he isn't, Parric thought, somebody else will have to kill him.

Chapter 13

"According to my all-knowing, pace of the Prophet's heart memory, we should get to the Central sometime tomorrow, assuming that it hasn't been blown off the face of the globe, and assuming no one tried to stop us from our sacred mission. If anyone wants to bet, let me know. I could use the money."

Parric nodded automatically, resigned and depressed by the foundation of skepticism upon which McLeod had, all morning, constructed his feeble forays into humor. The disillusionment had come swiftly and he had been struggling with it since leaving the Town: the search for the reason why he had thought his friend would have been as enthusiastic as he, and as dedicated. Two women and a dead man caught in his wake, showered by the chips of his molding of a dream, and McLeod was going to help him varnish that dream with shining reality. He shook his head and stared at the steep wall of the mountain blurring green and brown past the landcar. He was tired, fought to keep from dozing in the fear that should he sleep the landcar would be turned around and running back to the dubious shelter of an artificial Town.

And fear, he knew finally and sadly, was what kept McLeod from lending him total support.

Sometime during the night, after Jessica had slept and Peg was still trying to make up her mind, Parric had sat up in the realization that there would be for him never another Everlasting, that no matter what the outcome, he could never again allow himself to be anonymous.

I can't go out there again, Peg had said earlier.

Well, I'm going, damn it, and I need my sleep, McLeod had said as he stormed in from the bedroom to quiet the argument Peg had been nurturing between herself and Jessica. You can stay if you want to, but for my bleeding heart's sake, please let me sleep.

You'd leave me here all alone?

Nonsense. We'll leave Willard here to take care of you.

I can't stay here with that thing all by myself. He'll kill me.

No, Parric had thought after abdicating his leg of the debate, you'll kill yourself, and the hell of it will be, you'll live to regret it.

So, McLeod said, come along and be killed with your friends.

There had been a deep-sleep whimpering that kept him awake until dawn, and when Peg joined him in the kitchen to pack some food, he only smiled when she said she would go, smiled and said nothing as they crawled into the newer, more spacious landcar McLeod had wheeled out of the Central. Watching, however,

McLeod's nervousness as he sped past the deadened barrier. "It's not like we're going back, Cam," he'd said, and ached at the shuddering as McLeod struggled to believe.

Fear. Parric had ripped out the umbilical and was growing again, but Cam still had the nightmare of returning to prison. It was, to him, somehow still a dream or a minor vacation from Time's mainstream. He was afraid of being yanked back into the company of the whitecoats.

Why is it always me, Parric thought, who has to be strong? Who the hell died and made me God?

And as they traveled, several times the road turned to paving and was studded with lighting poles that on the straightaways seemed like disjointed bars on a long, narrow cage. Once in a while they stopped at a comunit exchange booth, but none were working, and when the facilities began appearing too close together, and signs for walkways began taking up space, McLeod shuffled through his memory and cut off the main route into secondary, untreated roads.

For the past three hours, then, as the mountains introduced themselves while scratching the sky, they had seen nothing but trees and some lackluster flowers.

Talk spurted, but Dix remained silent; he was directly behind Parric, Jessica in the middle, Peg on the left, and when she haltingly tried to apologize to him, the android said he didn't know what she was talking about.

"Looks easier to handle than the one we stole," Parric said once.

"Honest goods makes honest working," McLeod said, constantly releasing one hand or the other from the streamlined cuffs to rub at the stubble-shadow covering his head like a prickly cowl.

"You sure you know where you're going?" Jessica said, leaning forward to poke her head between the two front seats.

"M'dear, this handsome vehicle which, may I say with humiliating modesty, I arranged for a mighty good price—"

"And a few good bribes," Parric muttered, ignored.

"—has unerring directional capabilities which will enable it to find any line you care to draw between here and Panasia, rest her evil soul. In addition, may the seraphim pluck their little heartstrings for me, I have many times studied the route to the Central in case I had to journey there for emergencies."

"Liar," Parric said. "The only reason you'd want to go there would be to personally count your credits before they banked them for you."

"No faith, Frankie, no faith. However, be that as it may, I still know the way, and there lies your trust, I trust. The only thing I don't know for sure is what's in store between here and there."

"If it was a woman, you'd stop in a firestorm."

"Cam," Peg said, "are you one of those kind?"

McLeod tried to explain how he absolutely was not one of those kind, turned it into a mocking denunciation of Parric's hermitage, and Parric grinned relief to his reflection in the side-door glass.

"Hey," Jessica said, "don't look now, but there's life down there."

The road had been skirting a narrow valley violated only by a warped silver-blue ribbon of river; abruptly, however, it forked, McLeod taking the right to remain on the mountain while the left dropped and disappeared, snaking into view on the valley floor to become the main street of a fair-sized village. Swearing at the sun's glare on the water, Peg finally guessed it to be perhaps the second her mediteam had visited.

"It looks so quiet, though," she said, pressing close to the glass and pausing long enough for Parric to remember Eisentor. "Wait! I think I can see some people, though it could be my imagination."

"No, it isn't," Parric said after convincing himself McLeod wasn't going to drop them over for an unscheduled visit. "And if I'm not mistaken, it looks like they've set up some barriers in the road at either end. Can't make out what they've used, though."

Jessica confirmed Parric's guess, then waved her hands in frustration as her fingers sought the familiar grip of a long-lensed tricorder.

"Bet they're real friendly," Dix said, making Peg jump.

"Hey, let's go down there and see," she said.

"Forget it, little nurse," McLeod said, speeding up to put the village behind them. "Blockades mean only trouble for anyone trying to get in. Or out. Those folks down there do not want company of any kind. And I wouldn't be surprised if they had the guns to prove it."

"Just like those," Parric said quietly, straightening in his seat as he indicated with a nod the obstruction at the next bend.

There were three men standing in front of an overturned hovercat, their faces shielded by black, broadbrimmed hats and their hands resting lightly on the barrels of open stock ContiGuard rifles. They were not, however, wearing uniforms, only the tight, blotched costumes of hunters.

McLeod slowed, eased the landcar to a halt with its blunted nose aimed at a narrow gap between the mountainside and the 'cat. Parric looked once into the back of the car with a silent command, then tried to relax when one of the guards pushed himself away from his companions and walked carefully to McLeod's side, his rifle pointing at the ground, a finger filling the trigger guard. Cam pulled aside the front window and nodded, smiling and mopping at his scalp.

"Hot work," he said, trying to smooth the roughness of his voice. "All that sun's bad for the skin, so says the Allah-Be."

The man stooped to look inside. "Nicer out here than it is in there," he said, grinning, his free hand idly rubbing his chest. "You going somewhere special?"

"Away," Parric said before McLeod could answer. "Saved our freetime to do some walking. Heard over by Oraton what had happened and we really don't want to head back for Philayork until things cool down."

"You'll be gone for a long time," the man said, leaning against the car. "You heard about Eisentor?"

Parric nodded. "Heard about it, didn't see it. Doesn't look like you got hurt, though."

"Some doctors come in from the hospital and jabbed us a while back. Strangers, though, we don't know about."

"Are you from that town back there in the valley?" Jessica asked.

The man nodded. "Not them, though," he said, pointing. "One's from Foxhole, the other's living in Wedley."

"How come you're together?"

The man ducked down again and stared at her. Parric twisted slowly to brace one foot against the door. McLeod, he could see, was toying with the accelerator; he hadn't yet put on the emergency brake.

"Lady, you've been gone a while, that's for sure. This is Quilly country now. He got us rifles, a mess of good food, and told us what— Where did you say you was going?"

"As far away from this mess as possible," McLeod said.

"Well, be sure you don't go too far. When it comes dark, find a town to put up in. Don't know what crazies might be hidden back in the mountains, you know. Just this morning we got word about an andy group that was hitting some of the smaller places. If it weren't for men like Quilly, you folks wouldn't last a minute out here at night."

McLeod nodded and the women made appropriate noises of deep gratitude.

"Well, you get stuck for food or something," the man said, backing away, waving at the others, "come on back. We'll be glad to let you stay a while."

"We'll do that," McLeod said, letting the landcar roll slowly forward while the barricade vehicle was swiveled out of the way. "You men be careful now," he added, waving.

The man grinned, one finger polishing the mouth of the barrel, and it was all Parric could do to keep from putting his foot down on the accelerator.

"Quilly?" Peg said when several kilometers allowed them easy breathing.

"Some local businessman or politician, most likely," Jessica said. "Didn't waste much time carving himself out a little kingdom, did he?"

"Damned ambitious, too," McLeod said, straining to keep the car from drifting over the edge of the road as he pushed it as fast as the terrain would allow. "If he can get guns like that, he sure doesn't want to stop with

187

a valleyful of villages. I'll bet he's already drawing maps with his name all over them.''

"Why didn't they search us?" Peg said.

"No need," Dix said, startling Parric. "No danger."

"Since it's obvious we aren't plague-ridden, we're probably considered harmless city idiots who'll kill ourselves trying to run away. They're probably laughing their fool heads off right now.''

"I don't like it," Peg persisted. "You'd think they'd be more suspicious.''

"Thank your stars in orbit for little favors," McLeod said, "and pass something up here to eat. Unless anyone had any real objections, except for using nature's choicest bathroom, I don't really want to stop again.''

Parric agreed immediately and, after finishing his meal, tried to curl up on his seat to get some sleep. If they were going to drive all night, one of them should be at least awake enough to keep the landcar on the road. Sighing, he rested his head against the side door, felt the vehicle's vibrations, and tried to ignore them; they were insistent, however, and plowed furrows of headache from his forehead to the base of his skull. He heard McLeod humming tunelessly and tried to fashion a melody, shifted angrily, and cupped a hand between his head and the glass. Peg began a game, cajoling out of Jessica a desultory effort to name all the pre-Noram Presidents. Parric counted to himself to block out the noise, daydreamed pictures of his office and looked for the names of the men who had worked there; what he saw instead was the Secretary rolling between the narrow aisles, sweeping from the seats the remains of a thousand clerks who had died counting premiums.

"Damn," he said, sitting straight again, brushing

188

his forearm across his face. "Want me to drive a little, Cam?"

McLeod shook his head. "In a bit, maybe, but not now. I need something to do, if you know what I mean."

"Absolutely," Parric said.

"Let's trade life stories," said Peg.

Jessica laughed, and when Parric turned to stare at the nurse, he wondered at the doe-fear in her eyes.

"No, really, if we're going to be with one another for a long time, wouldn't it be a good idea to know the other person as well as you can?" She frowned. "Do you know what I mean?"

"Sure," Parric said, "and if you don't mind, I'd just as soon read about myself in Jessica's history, about a million years from now."

"You're no fun, Frank," she said.

"Maybe," Jessica said, "but he's got a point. Time machines may be all right for some people, but we've got no use for them now. The past, I hate to remind you, isn't what you think it was, and a lot deader."

"More dead," Parric said.

"Whatever," Jessica said.

"You're no fun either, Jess," Peg said and twisted her lips into a pout that made them both laugh.

"Ah, party time," McLeod said, "but it looks like there's more damned roadblocks in this area than there are trees. Here we go again, fellow travelers."

Parric quieted, though a grin remained, and for a minute thought they'd been riding in a vast circle. For the second time a landcar obstructed the road, and again three men in hunter's garb and broad-brimmed hats stood waiting for them. When their vehicle stopped, nothing moved.

"They want us to get out?" McLeod said.

"Forget it," Parric said. "If they want information, they'll have to come and get it."

"What about him?" McLeod said, jerking his head back toward a silent Dix.

Parric didn't turn around. "You're still alive," he said quietly.

An hour-long minute, then one guard propped his rifle against the blockade debris and removed his hat, slapping it against his legs as he walked toward the car. He was young, younger than Parric, but there was a coarseness about his eyes that suggested aging wood. He rapped on the windshield with his knuckles and beckoned, but McLeod only smiled and slid open the window.

"Trouble?" he asked politely.

"Just want you folks out of that car," the young man said as if inviting them out for dinner. "Don't want you baking in there while we talk."

"What's to talk? We're only heading into the mountains away from the plague and stuff," McLeod said as Parric tried not to be conspicuous tripping the lever that locked his side of the car.

"From the city, huh?"

"Philayork," McLeod said. "We were vacationing—"

"I know, I know," the man said. "Going to do some walking. Going to hide in the hills until the world comes back, right?"

Parric frowned, shrugged when Cam looked to him for an answer. Though he hadn't seen it, there was apparently some sort of comlink between roadblocks, and the first had obviously become suspicious.

"Tell you what, mister," the man said, smiling.

190

"Why don't you shut this thing down a minute. Can't hardly hear you over that whining."

"Well, it's been giving me some trouble lately," McLeod stalled. "I don't know if I could start it again."

"Don't you worry about it. I got a friend standing right over there who's a great mechanic. He can start anything that has an engine. Please, shut it down."

Parric tensed, waiting to see if McLeod would try to run the blockade, but the pair remaining in front of them had shifted their weapons to their hips, muzzles down but unmistakably at the ready; and after a long count of five, he reached over and flicked off the ignition. He looked and saw Jessica pressed close to Dix, but Peg was leaning forward, grinning broadly, and he cursed her stupidity. Neutral was what they should be, not engaging or provocative.

The man tapped on the door impatiently until McLeod shrugged off the cuffs and hiked up the door, cocking it perpendicular to the roof of the car.

"Very good," the man said. "Now I can see you all better. Say, you must have a pretty good plant in there, you're not sweating a bit. That's a shame because my friends and I have been standing out here since early this morning and there's damned little shade, you can believe me. Tell you what: so you won't get them angry at being so comfortable, why don't you step outside and say hello?"

"No, thanks," McLeod said. "My legs, you know," and he gestured vaguely toward the floor, never completed the motion as the man grabbed his shoulders and yanked him clear. Instantly, McLeod was on his feet and had his arms wrapped around the other's waist, his momentum slamming both of them against the hood and off onto the ground. Parric, his door lever jammed, scrambled over the seats to the outside, but his intentions to assist Cam were stifled when he saw the guards aiming carefully at his and the others' heads.

And except for the grunting, it was silent, silence lightly edged with ragged fearful breathing.

A moment later, McLeod was dragged to his feet and shoved against the car. He fell halfway in, was yanked out and pushed toward Parric, who grabbed his arms to steady him.

"Didn't notice your *hero* trying to save us this time," McLeod whispered harshly.

"He didn't turn on you, either," Parric snapped. "In case you've forgotten, there are four of us."

The man wiped his face, brushed at his trousers, and scanned the ground for his hat, finding it behind the front wheel. He was grinning in spite of welling bruises on his right cheek, and nodded as he tried to comb the dirt from his hair with his fingers.

"Well, you do come out when you're told," he said. "I got to say that much. But why jump me? I mean, what have I done?"

"Bastard," McLeod said despite Peg's tugging at his arm. "If I wasn't so tired from driving—"

"Oh, probably," the man said, "but right now you are and I'm not, so let's be friends, all right?"

"Friends?" Peg said. "What are you going to do, rob us?"

"Not me," he said, looking insulted. "I'm no thief, I'm a soldier."

"Then where's your uniform?"

"Don't have one, little lady. I don't belong to the

192

ContiGuard, if that's what's in your mind. I'm in Quilly's army.''

"Never heard of him." Her folded arms emphasized her disdain. .

"You will. Now I want you to follow Mark over there. He's going to put you all up for the night.''

"Frank!" she said, but he only shook his head and pointed to the raised rifles.

"Frank!"

"Hush, damn it!" McLeod said, taking her arm and pulling. "Do you want to get me killed?''

Parric heard them arguing, wanted to shut them up, but the man called Mark was walking only a few paces to his right, leading them off the road and down a winding, stepped trail toward, he could see through the trees, a village larger than the one they had seen earlier. Twice Jessica tried to goad their guard into talking, but she received nothing more than a general, menacing swing of his weapon. "Five against one," he heard Peg say to McLeod in a ludicrous attempt at whispering, but when he turned around he saw Cam jerking a thumb over his shoulder toward the road above where the two remaining guards were watching them through their rifles' sights. Suddenly Peg began to cry and McLeod, from anger to comforter, hugged her close and didn't let go until they had quit the trees and found themselves in a small park behind a two-story fieldstone building. Eisentor, Parric though instantly as he looked past the circular flowerbeds to the ordered streets beyond. He smiled, then, at Jess whose shivering led him to believe she'd received the same impression, but winced when the man called Mark jabbed his knee with his rifle and pointed to the side of the building.

"Up the stairs, first room, they're waiting on you," he said, pushing aside a heavy metal door.

"It talks," McLeod said, and glared back when the guard stared angrily at him.

"Come on, old man, move it!" Mark snapped, pushing Dix in behind Parric and Jessica. "I haven't got all day."

"Brave, too," McLeod said, and when the rifle was swung in his direction, he grabbed the barrel, yanked, and threw it across the street. He nodded once, waited a moment before closing the door in the man's face and running up the short flight of steps to join Peg.

"Could have been killed," Dix said without turning around.

McLeod was silent for a moment. "You going to tell me you care?"

"Yep."

"Damn," he said. "I wish . . ."

Parric waited until they'd reached the small landing, too numbed by their sudden capture to do more than follow instructions. It would have been foolhardy for anything else, he realized, since anyone in this town could instantly brand them strangers and ask questions he probably could not answer.

The room they entered was large, one of the biggest Parric had ever seen. A full ten meters on a side, it was virtually without furniture except for a battered conference table in its center. There were four chairs spaced irregularly around it, and on the walls nothing but the yellow and gray that had crept in yearly to discolor the paint.

"Not bad," McLeod said, walking around. "Wish it had windows, though. I'd like to see what the rest of the place looks like."

"Not me," said Jessica. "I just want out."

"Why?" Peg said. "They're not going to rob or kill us. Maybe they just want to know about where we came from. Maybe they're just nervous we might be carrying the plague or something. You know, enemy spies?"

"Maybe," Parric said, "but I doubt it. I had been thinking it would be silly to try anything, but now I've changed my mind. Some or all, we've got to get to the Central."

"You worry too much," Dix said, sitting at the head of the table. "When we find out, doc, then we do something."

"Is he always right?" McLeod said.

Parric shrugged, thinking incongruously of the song Dix had wanted him to like almost a light-year ago, and he was about to ask him to sing it when the door opened and several oddly uniformed men entered. They were all armed to one degree or another, and none of them smiled like the guard on the road.

Chapter 14

Parric awakened with his skull embroiled in a volcanic eruption. He sobbed and clutched at his hair as if to tear it out.

Who are you, Mr. Parric?

I told you who I was. Franklin Parric. From Philayork. My friends and I were out on a vacation when the war news broke. We—

You said that already, Mr. Parric. But you haven't answered my question. Who are you, Mr. Parric? And who are your friends?

It was dark, too dark to see even his hands when he pressed them against his cheek to keep his teeth from rattling to the floor. He was leaning against a wall, his legs twisted behind him. He tasted blood and spat, and when he felt he would no longer vomit, he placed a hand on the surface beneath him, and it was earth, and damp.

If you've been traveling as long as you say, Mr. Parric, why isn't your landcar more dirty? Did you stop often to clean it? I've heard you city people are a cleanly lot, but I didn't think it would extend to lengthy trips in the country.

What town is this?

We're thinking about renaming it, Mr. Parric, so its former title will have no meaning for you. Especially if you're from the city and wouldn't know it anyway.

I told you a hundred times, I'm from—

Philayork and you work as a clerk in some ridiculous insurance company. All right, Mr. Parric, that much I can believe—

—then how about letting me out of this. What have I done, for crying out loud?

You? Probably nothing, Mr. Parric, but we are interested in your friends. You see, there was a mediteam in here not too long ago that supposedly took care of our needs concerning that war you said you heard about. Well, Mr. Parric, that mediteam was a sham. We had a lot of people die rather horribly around here.

Minutes later the aching subsided, burrowing worm-like but not forgotten. He passed his hands around him on the floor, looking for clues, finding nothing but dirt, dampness, and the stench of his lunch. With his teeth grinding, he pushed himself up against the wall, stood, but carefully since the lack of light threatened his balance, and for a long and vertiginous moment he felt as if he were falling slowly into a wide-mouthed well. A sudden shift and he was convinced he was standing on a narrow ledge. He flattened himself against the wall and edged along its base, his hands spread to either side. It took him a while to realize the wall was constructed of wood, roughly cut, perhaps even unpainted.

When he came to the first corner he stopped, reached above him, then squatted to examine the floor, stood, and moved again, counting this time to give him an estimate of the room's size, something, anything to lend substance to the well that threatened to suck him under.

Listen, whoever you are—are you Quilly, by any chance?

Now be honest, Mr. Parric. Do you think Quilly would bother with innocent travelers just passing through his country?

His country? What the hell kind of talk is that? This is Noram, and I suggest you don't forget it.

Noram? My dear Mr. Parric, Noram was, not is. Things have changed since you've been gone, sir, and may I suggest you don't cling to the old ways too long or you could easily get yourself hurt.

Look, mister, I really don't know what's going on around here, and I'd appreciate it if you'd fill me in. And while you're at it, you might tell me what's happened to my friends.

The second and third walls were the same: blank, splinter filled, and much taller than he could reach. Several times he stopped, turned to face what he thought was the room's center, and stared, trying to find cracks of light that would guide him to a window or a door. But there was nothing but the gnatlights in his head that confused and dizzied him. He considered the possibility of being in a below-ground cell of some sort with no entrance but a trap in the ceiling; but he dismissed it immediately it occurred to him, not for the implausability but for the desperation that would immobilize him when he would be unable to reach the exit. He moved again, slowly, his hands lightly brushing the wall, tender nevertheless and beginning to sting. And when, in an overhead movement, his fingers traced the metal outline of a pinned hinge, he had to bite the insides of his cheeks to keep from shouting.

Nothing has happened to them, Mr. Parric. They are as well-kept as you, perhaps even better.

If you call being tied to a chair ten sizes too small well-kept, then I hope to hell they're better.

You're short-tempered, Mr. Parric, a trait which will get us nowhere. Now, if you please, who are you and where are you coming from?

You must be deaf.

I understand perfectly what you told me, Mr. Parric. What I want now is the truth.

I gave you that, too, but apparently our definitions aren't quite the same.

Obviously.

What's that?

A needle, Mr. Parric. I should have thought of this before.

What are you going to do?

Now don't get hysterical, Mr. Parric. I'm only going to draw a little blood. That is, if you have any.

You're kidding. You mean to tell me you think I'm—

—an android? Could be, Mr. Parric. Stranger things have happened since the war, you know. Stories, if you know what I mean. About bands of superhuman men rampaging around the countryside raping women and burning little children to death. Tearing men apart

with their bare hands, that sort of thing. The usual exaggerated nightmares, I suppose, but they do have some basis in fact.

What makes you think that?

Why, Mr. Parric, we've killed a couple ourselves, right here in town. They tried to pass for human. Can you imagine that? Tell me, Mr. Parric, and it won't hurt a bit, are your friends human, too?

There was no disappointment when he found the door locked, but a genuine shudder of relief that his earlier fear of an underground cell could be buried without mourning. He listened for what he hoped was a long time, time now being nothing without a watch or light by which to measure it. Listened, hearing nothing but his own labored breathing, his own blood pounding to get him out. That the door was hinged gave him a much better chance to escape than a regular exit, and when he found the knob he pulled steadily until his arms ached at the shoulders. He stopped, listened again, then tried a series of quick jerks, each more frantic than the last, until he slumped onto the floor and tried not to cry. Without tools he could not hope to pry off the hinges or rip out the lock; without light, he couldn't hope to find what weaknesses the door had except by touch alone, and his hands were too sore to be reliable. He crawled around on the floor, then, searching for something to use, one hand brushing over the dirt, the other held stiffly in front of him to guard against striking a wall. And there was nothing, not even a rock thin enough to be of some use. He sat, the walls somewhere beyond him, and began delving into his clothes. He knew there was nothing there, but he had to be sure, and in searching found a triangular piece of metal and glass tucked deep in a pocket.

Mr. Parric, we might as well be honest with each other. We're not quite as primitive as some of our young men would lead you to believe. There was a link between our roadblocks—

—I gathered that. So what?

So, Mr. Parric, it seems that one of the ladies with whom you are so innocently traveling was part of the mediteam that thought it was helping us. You look surprised.

I didn't think anyone recognized doctors, especially when they're too busy doling out shots.

This particular lady is most striking, you have to admit, Mr. Parric, and as she is part and complete a factor in our troubles, naturally we wanted to meet her again. And just as naturally we wanted to meet her friends.

I don't understand. If you were inoculated, how did you get the plague?

Oh, we're working on that, Mr. Parric, believe me. The best our local medicine men have come up with for the moment is that the synthidote was not entirely pure to begin with. Perhaps haste in its manufacture, perhaps something inherent in its basic structure. At any rate, Mr. Parric, it didn't work for all of us, and needless to say we are not very happy about it.

You could at least be thankful you're not Eisentor.

We could be, and we are, Mr. Parric, but that hardly changes matters, does it?

He thought and remembered: in carrying Jessica out of the Town where Ike had been killed, he was the one who had opened the barriers, had thought he had returned the patchkey to Jessica, which caused him to blame her when they could not immediately get into McLeod's Town. When he had changed clothes, he had absently transferred his pockets' contents without checking them. He wanted to see himself smiling, hugged himself instead, and it was Time again as he searched the walls for the door, then waited a millennium until nerve regrouped and he felt for the gap between the lock housing and the frame. And when he found it he breathed. Carefully he slid the key against the bolt and tried to push it back into the door. The key slid twice along the bolt before it caught, and moved, but not enough. He beat back frustration and tried again.

A simple matter of justice, Mr. Parric.
Nonsense.
You're a rather brave man for one in your position.
Stand me up and I'll show you how shitless I'm scared, mister, but that doesn't change things for me, either. If what you say is true, then—
Oh, please, Mr. Parric, stop playing with me. You forget I make up the rules here.
If what you say is true, then you're considering the rest of us guilty by association.
That's a good way to put it, Mr. Parric.
And what happens to us?
We have three choices: we could kill you all right now and be done with it. We could detain you indefinitely as an example to those few remaining recalcitrants who aren't exactly taken with Quilly's, shall we say, presence? Or we could let you go free and forget all about you.

I prefer the last one, if you don't mind. The other two are senseless.

Senseless, Mr. Parric, only when you're not trying to prove something.

Are you?

Not me, Mr. Parric, but Quilly certainly is. Absolutely. I think, Mr. Parric, the phrase is: I'll see you at dawn.

The door opened slowly as Parric stuffed the patch-key back into his pocket and stood to one side. There was light, dim but bright enough to momentarily blind him. Without looking back, he stepped out and closed the door. He was in a hall cluttered with unidentifiable pieces of machinery, split and warped lumber, and plastiboard cartons piled in unsteady rows to the ceiling. At a junction some twenty meters away was a small bulb fastened to the wall and a second corridor running at right angles to the first. There were no other doors that he could see, no guards or sensing devices readily apparent. Picking his way over the litter, he managed to reach the light without undue noise. He waited a moment, listening, sniffing once at the nausea clinging to him before looking around the corner. A maze, it seemed to him. To the left was another bulb marking yet another junction, to the right a triple fork, and no doors or lights. The silence began to fade into faint background sounds of gurgling pipes, floorboards trod upon above him and, closer, someone crying. To the left, and he saw a door similar to the one he had just jimmied; and again, no guards. He smiled at his captors' self-confidence, trusted in their continued faith as he entered the new hall and crept to the door. Knocking once, lightly, twice, once, he tried the knob, found it

203

locked, and freed it with the patchkey. Jessica stood blinking at him before accepting his arms and clinging with her own before he led her away. There was no conversation, he permitted none until retreating to his own hall and pressing his lips against her ear to ask if she knew where the others were. She shook her head, then pointed past her own cell and shrugged. He thought, then led the way to the next corner, the next door, and Dix, who was sitting in the middle of the floor, humming.

Parric watched the android rocking, wondering if he had been discovered, but when he called in a whisper, Dix turned and smiled, rose and followed.

Several times, in the labyrinth of the underground prison, they found themselves retracing their steps, finding their footprints in layers of dust, seeing the junk they had pushed aside to clear their way. Many passages were impassable, two others blocked by solid metal doors that stymied breaching. Parric began to fear becoming hopelessly lost, entrapped by his own daring in a warren to which he was a stranger. For half an hour they crouched against a wall listening to sounds of increased activity directly above them, a great deal of running and, finally, muffled shouts. When it quieted, they moved cautiously again, this time trying to follow the sounds' direction, and in following, discovered a staircase.

"Choice," Parric whispered, the word echoing unpleasantly in his ear. "We try for the Central and bring back help, or we risk getting caught and find Peg and Cam."

"No choice," Dix said and led the way up before Jessica could answer. Parric stared at the android's back, then pushed her in front of him. There was a door at the top and the beat of one man walking behind it. Down the hall were wooden steps still climbing, and Jessica watched them while Dix bent to find a way to see into the room. When he straightened, he shook his head, took hold of the knob, and wrenched it. A scream of metal exploded in the dim corridor and Parric tried not to clamp his hands over his ears. The door swung in and Dix was gone before he could be stopped. Jessica and Parric didn't hesitate charging in after him and saw him sitting on the floor with a man, the one they called Mark, trapped in the net of his arms.

Parric made sure he wouldn't call out, then hurried to the oval window at the front. The street, as far as he could see, was deserted, but house lights and street-lamps kept the evening at bay and banished the outlines of the mountains.

"Where are they?" Parric said, kneeling in front of the man.

Mark shook his head as best he could in the vise of the android's grip.

"Oh, I'm sure you know," Parric said, remembering the needles of his interrogator, "and I'm just as sure you're going to tell me. You see, this man here trying to separate your head from your shoulders isn't a man after all. He's an android."

Mark's eyes widened, tried to look up as Dix practiced an evil-sounding chuckle.

"He's also quite mad, and I'm the only one who can control him."

"Come on, Frank," Jessica said impatiently. "Somebody's bound to hear us before too long."

"She's right, you know," Parric said, "and if they

find us alive, that's something you won't be. Where are they?''

He nodded for Dix to loosen his grip, his own hand cupped near Mark's throat to strangle should a cry escape, but the young guard was too frightened, too eager to be free of the android, to do anything but cower and massage his neck.

"Outside," he said finally, choking. "They took the little guy and that woman outside."

"Where? Why?"

"I don't know why." Parric threatened with a look to Dix. "The girl will probably get shot or something," Mark said quickly. "I don't know about the bald guy. Maybe they just want some fun, you know what I mean? Quilly sometimes lets us do that if—"

He shut up when Parric stood and rushed back to the window. "You have a cat or a landcar?"

Mark nodded, now only too eager to please. "Landcar in the alley outside. A cat's not much good in the mountains."

"Keys," Jessica snapped, holding our her hand. The man reached awkwardly into his hip pocket, pulled out a small case, and tossed it to her when she gestured. "How long ago did they leave?"

"Just a couple of minutes, honest. Hey, look, you're going to let me go, aren't you? I won't say anything, really. I don't want any trouble."

"Come on, Frank," she said. "We haven't got much time."

"Right," he said. "Someone's coming down the street. Willard, do something to keep him quiet, then follow us in a hurry."

He grabbed Jessica's hand and left the roof, almost running to the side of the building, but not fast enough to avoid hearing the half-scream choked off and buried. Jessica slammed open the only door in sight and was out without looking to see if anyone was watching. Parric, with Dix right behind him, joined her and found himself in an alley, a landcar parked ahead facing the street.

"That must be it."

Jessica nodded.

"Well," he said, noting the space between the vehicle and the buildings on either side, "he sure doesn't have wing doors."

"You buying or stealing?" she said and, when he looked at her, smiled.

"You I'm going to teach some manners someday," he said. They ran to the car, used the keys to open the back hatch, and clambered in. Dix sat up front with Parric while Jessica crouched on the floor behind them. And once out of the alley, Parric could see movement several blocks ahead, small groups of people mingling, splitting, meeting again. Slowly he rode a sidestreet parallel to the activity, knowing what was planned and amazed to see people sitting on their porches or strolling along the sidewalks as if nothing at all untoward were happening.

"Callous bastards," he said at one intersection.

"Survival," Dix said.

"Maybe," Parric said.

He guessed by their direction and the increasing density of houses that the building in which they had been imprisoned was close to the village's limits, became positive they would find Cam and Peg somewhere near the center, perhaps at some ritual meeting-place where Quilly passed his law.

"Can't you hurry?" Jessica said.

"Hurry! I don't even know where I'm going."

"Try there," Dix said, pointing to an intersection centered with a dead stoplight.

Parric turned left and encountered the fringe of a minor traffic jam. Landcars and hissing hovercats were pressing on all sides in the one-way street, heading right around the next corner. When Parric reached it, his hands beginning to slicken the rims of the cuffs, he saw a small crowd gathering haphazardly near the entrance to a ContiGov market.

"Don't stop," Dix warned, and Parric reluctantly agreed, knowing if they abandoned the landcar now, they'd never get back to it in time should they manage to reach and rescue their friends. A man crossing the street in front of him stopped for a moment and stared. Parric smiled and waved, the man waved hesitantly back and moved out of his way.

"Floyd is never going to believe this," Jessica said, sitting up and staring at the scene outside the car. "Not even from me will he believe this."

"Why? What's so special about you?" Parric said, faking another smile at a group of elderly pedestrians.

"My dad, you know," she said.

"Can't be," Parric said. "Your name is Windsor."

"Archaic custom, clerk," she said. "Keep the name of your late husband."

He almost braked, frustrated at the timing of her news, shook off the impulse, and stared as he passed into the front of the store. The windows had been removed and there was a low platform erected just inside where ration displays had once been. It was empty, but by the agitation of the onlookers it wouldn't be for very long.

And six armed hunters flanked a man Parric recognized as his tormentor.

"There!" Dix said suddenly, finally betraying excitement, pointing as Parric reached the far corner ready to dispair at their next move.

A half a block away, led and followed by a grinning, obviously anxious honor guard were Cam and Peg, their legs free but their hands bound behind their backs. They stumbled over nothings and their faces were streaked an ugly dark. The people who were waiting for whatever show had been planned had not yet seen them and before Parric understood what he was doing, he sped up, jumped the curb, and aimed straight for them. The guards, initially frozen in disbelief, suddenly scattered to safety, most of them sprawling into the street or under parked vehicles. Parric grunted as the steering fought him, braked hard when he came abreast of the prisoners, gunning the engine as Jessica flung up the hatch and grabbed for Peg's pinioned arms. Cam blinked puzzlement until Dix shouted, then butted Peg in the back and jumped in after her as two of the guards, quicker than the others, unholstered hand weapons and began firing. Cam moaned and Peg cried out, but the landcar was off the sidewalk and into the street heading out of the village before the rest could react effectively.

Parric could only stare, then, watching the houses streak past, once closing his eyes at an intersection where he ignored a red warning light. He listened above the car's protesting whine for bays of pursuit, but there was nothing, nothing at all but a roadblock ahead, which he squeezed past without slowing down, grimacing at the thud of a body that did not quite jump aside in time.

Driving while a woman cried.

Piercing darkness while a man grunted agony.

His hands began to shake and the car began to sway.

He barely heard Dix telling him to slow down, barely aware that the android was guiding him to their destination.

Chapter 15

There was, finally, peace.

"Your father, huh?"

"That's right."

"Why didn't you tell me?"

"You never asked."

"I asked you a hundred times what the story was with you, damn it, but you never gave me a straight answer."

"I don't think I would have, either, at least not for a while. He's an incurable matchmaker, you see, and I don't think I wanted to give him the satisfaction."

"I think that's a compliment."

"Don't let it go to your head, clerk."

They had climbed the low hill that swelled the east end of the Central, were watching the streets fill with people taking an afternoon break from the painful business of survival. Low and ragged clouds kept the scene from being as bright as it could have been, but neither Parric nor Jessica were looking for omens.

"No androids yet," Jessica said.

Parric shook his head. And there wouldn't be for

some time. Most of the Central's original simulacra had succumbed to the plague and had been quickly destroyed. Less than a dozen prototypes, of which Dix had been one, were under intense experimentation and would not be released until their sanity could be guaranteed. Once that was accomplished, and Coates left no doubt that it would be, survivors such as McLeod would have to have their lingering doubts exorcised. It had dismayed Parric during the first few days to realize that the people he'd counted on to bring reason back to the world would have to be the first to be conquered.

Dismay, however, had finally turned the corner to optimism.

A cloud-shadow passed over him and he shuddered.

"I went by to check on Cam and Peg this morning."

Jessica nodded absently. "Floyd's been locking me up until I get all those reporters' impressions down. I'll try to get to them this afternoon if I can."

"Well, Cam is doing fine considering all the yelling he's doing, and the new curses he's thought up for the mediunits and doctors. His hip will be strong enough to carry his weight in a week or two, but his insides aren't responding as fast. He says it's a conspiracy to keep him from going back and strangling Quilly."

"I think they're going to let him try."

"I believe it. Peg's hand, by the way, is only bandaged. She spends most of her time gaging Cam."

"It seems lonely without them."

"It does," he said, and lonelier still when he thought of the reality brought to the dream he had had. Central had been the paradise, somehow immune from the plague and miraculously untouched by the panic and violence still awash in the country. But Central was, in fact, only human, and being human, afraid. Though the

ContiGov had suffered more Cabinet casualties than he'd suspected, it had not fled to a secret capital in the country's center but had, instead, debarked to the Central where it cast for a positive mold to shape the business of the future. Fear was the goad, determination the fuel, and Parric was just as adamant as anyone about his own role in the crisis.

Priorities: rest for himself easily attained, and a constant badgering of Coates not to shut the rest of the world out and allow insulation to poison the Central's thinking.

"I'll tell you one thing, Jess," he said, pulling at the grass and watching the streets empty again, "I'm not going to be a goddamned clerk again."

"What are you going to be . . . a general?"

He grinned. "Hardly, lady reporter, but I'll be damned if I'm going to sit behind a console while all this is going on. I've been talking with your father."

There was a silence, not strained but apprehensive.

"He mentioned something to me," she said softly. "I didn't have time to listen." Didn't want to, her tone said, and Parric pulled gently at her hair.

"There are things that have to be done, Jess. Teams to hunt out birds we can breed. Fast, before the insects make food production impossible. Teams to bring in people and towns, bring them back to ContiGov before what's left of the population fractures into kingdoms like Quilly's."

"There'll be fighting."

"And we'll need soldiers, too. And ways to reestablish comlinks and transportation. We may be back on horses in some places."

"Sometimes I wonder . . ."

"Don't!" he said sharply. "If we wonder, we'll lose."

"What about . . . the androids?"

"Them, too," he said, nodding. "Once Dix gets out of that lab with the others we'll have to produce more like them, take them out into the field with rehabilitation teams." He thought of Oraton and Eisentor. "That's what I want to do, Jess. That's what I am going to do. Coates is going to let me headman an expedition to Philayork to see what we can recover. Philayork, and other points east. They say I'm pretty good at getting androids accepted."

"Don't sound so smug, clerk. You may have convinced McLeod and Peggy, but the rest of them out there might not be so easy."

"Maybe. But I have to do something."

Again a silence, and Parric watched winds of expression move Jess' features into something that finally gave him buoyant hope.

"I know what you mean," she said. "I'm getting a little itchy myself. It's too damned quiet around here."

"I think Willard will go with me. He wants to, if I know him as well as I claim."

"Why, Frank?"

"I couldn't say for sure. Maybe he's afraid Cam will teach him to say more than five words in a sentence. Maybe he likes me. I don't know."

"I didn't mean that. I mean, why don't you play it safe and do what you can around here? God knows you deserve that much!"

"Now that's a loaded question, reporter, and you've already had enough answers to it."

"*Alpha?*"

"That's only part of it, now."

"So you're going to save the world, huh?"

"One way or another."

Shadows buried the houses beneath quiet trees, and as lights were turned on, the valley became a reflecting pool for the night sky.

"All right, clerk. Now I know what you mean. For history, right?"

"You got it, young lady. You got it."

THE BRIGHTEST STARS IN BERKLEY'S GALAXY
THE ALPHA AND OMEGA OF SCIENCE FICTION

GALACTIC POT-HEALER   (N2569—95¢)
  Philip K. Dick

THE MOUNTAINS OF THE SUN   (N2570—95¢)
  Christian Leourier

ORBIT 13   (N2698—95¢)
  ed. by Damon Knight

THE STARS MY DESTINATION   (Z2780—$1.25)
  Alfred Bester

NIGHTMARE BLUE   (N2819—95¢)
  Dozios & Effinger

PSTALEMATE   (N2962—95¢)
  Lester del Rey

THE COMPUTER CONNECTION   (D3039—$1.50)
  Alfred Bester

THE FLOATING ZOMBIE   (Z2980—$1.25)
  D.F. Jones

Send for a *free* list of all our books in print

These books are available at your local bookstore, or
send price indicated plus 30¢ per copy to cover mailing
costs to

Berkley Publishing Corporation
200 Madison Avenue
New York, New York 10016